Dear Reader,

The leaves aren't the only things changing colors this October. Starting this month, you'll notice Silhouette Intimate Moments is evolving into its vibrant new look, and that's just the start of some exciting changes we're undergoing. As of February 2007, we will have a new name, Silhouette Romantic Suspense. Not to worry, these are still the breathtaking romances—don't forget the suspense!—that you've come to know and love in Intimate Moments. Keep your eyes open for our new look over the next few months as we transition fully to our new appearance. As always, we deliver on our promise of romance, danger and excitement.

Speaking of romance, danger and excitement, award-winning author Ruth Wind brings us *Juliet's Law* (#1435), the debut of her miniseries SISTERS OF THE MOUNTAIN. An attorney must depend on a handsome tribal officer to prove her sister's innocence on murder charges. Wendy Rosnau continues her arresting SPY GAMES series with *Undercover Nightingale* (#1436) in which an explosives expert falls for an undercover agent and learns just how deceiving looks can be.

You'll nearly swoon as a Navajo investigator protects a traumatized photojournalist in *The Last Warrior* (#1437) by Kylie Brant. Don't miss Loreth Anne White's new miniseries, SHADOW SOLDIERS, and its first story, *The Heart of a Mercenary* (#1438), a gripping tale with a to-die-for alpha hero!

This month, and every month, let our stories sweep you into an exciting world of passion and suspense. Happy reading!

Sincerely,

Patience Smith
Associate Senior Editor

Please address questions and book requests to:
Silhouette Reader Service
U.S.: 3010 Walden Ave., P.O. Box 1325, Buffalo, NY 14269
Canadian: P.O. Box 609, Fort Erie, Ont. L2A 5X3

Wendy Rosnau

UNDERCOVER NIGHTINGALE

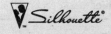

Silhouette

INTIMATE MOMENTS™

Published by Silhouette Books

America's Publisher of Contemporary Romance

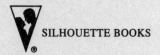

SILHOUETTE BOOKS

ISBN-13: 978-0-373-27506-9
ISBN-10:   0-373-27506-4

UNDERCOVER NIGHTINGALE

Copyright © 2006 by Wendy Rosnau

WENDY ROSNAU

resides on sixty secluded acres in Minnesota with her husband and their two children. She divides her time between her family-owned bookstore and writing romantic suspense.

Her first book, *The Long Hot Summer,* was a *Romantic Times BOOKclub* nominee for Best First Series Romance of 2000. Her third book, *The Right Side of the Law,* was a *Romantic Times BOOKclub* Top Pick. She received the Midwest Fiction Writers 2001 Rising Star Award.

Wendy loves to hear from her readers. Visit her Web site at www.wendyrosnau.com.

Prologue

Barinski was humming to himself, his black-rimmed glasses perched high on his protruding forehead when the Chameleon entered the soundproof cubicle in the bowels of the mosque.

Some people should never reproduce. That's what had come to mind the first day he had met Nigel Barinski. The peculiar-looking scientist was a mutation of bad genetics—arms that hung at his sides like an ape, and a pair of short legs to cement the concept. He had a receding chin, oversized ears, too much curly red hair, and a pair of unnatural glass-bowl goldfish eyes.

But appearance had nothing to do with intellect. In Barinski's case, the price for his gift of genius was his misshapen body and Frankenstein face.

The Chameleon dismissed Barinski for a moment

and focused on the woman on the other side of the two-way mirror strapped into Barinski's two-million-dollar chair, in what he called the regeneration chamber. Her eyes were closed, and she was calm, as if she was in a dream-like state. A much different story than when she'd first been brought to him.

"How is she progressing?"

"On schedule."

"No surprises?"

"None."

The Chameleon stepped closer to the window. He'd first seen her in Munich. She'd been scaling a fifty-foot wall, her curvy body suspended from a guide wire as if it was a part of her instead of her lifeline.

He'd never seen a woman with so much courage packaged so beautifully. He had found her bravery as arousing as her curves, and in that moment he knew he had to have her. Knew she would be the perfect guinea pig for Barinski's latest genius.

Barinski flipped a switch. "*Kalimera*, Nightingale."

She opened her eyes as if Barinski's voice had turned on a lightbulb inside her head. "Good morning."

"Did you sleep well?"

"Yes. I dreamt about Bonnie."

The Chameleon turned the switch off. "Who's Bonnie?"

"Her mother. A slut, from the information I've gathered."

"I don't care about her childhood, or her mother."

"You should. The scientific data on a child's adaptability into society parallels what they have been taught. It's one of the reasons you're so taken with

Nightingale. She's a product of suffering, and sacrifice. She knows how to survive."

"Because she hates her mother?"

"No, because she loves her. All children love their parents. Even when they hate them."

The Chameleon would have accepted Barinski's theory if he didn't have proof that on this particular point he was as crazy as he looked. His own daughter hated him, and it would take a miracle to change Melita's mind.

"Enough about children loving their parents even if they hate them," he said, then flipped the switch and spoke into the vibration grid that would distort his voice. "Do you remember Munich?"

She hesitated a moment. "I've never been to Munich."

"Brussels, how did you like it there?"

"I've never visited Brussels."

The Chameleon glanced at Barinski. "She really can't remember?"

"I've left her childhood recall intact, but the past six years are gone."

"Very good, Barinski."

Like a puppy whose head had just been patted, Barinski turned warm and fuzzy, his goofy grin making him look even more ridiculous.

"By the end of the week I'll start entering your data. If you want her to remember Munich, or a portion of what she's lost, she will. If not, she won't."

The Chameleon turned back to the two-way mirror and searched her eyes for the fire he remembered. It wasn't there. She was a blank canvas, and he was suddenly disappointed in that.

"You're sure once the procedure is complete that she'll function as before?" He turned to Barinski. "I don't want her ending up a damn freak."

There was a moment of silence. Obviously Dr. Frankenstein was touchy around the word "freak."

Barinski cleared his throat, and it sounded as if he was flushing a toilet. "She'll have the same advanced skills as before. I've been keeping her physical workouts short but intense, and she's on a special diet. A month to integrate her skills with your data and she'll be as dangerous as when she was captured. Only she'll be working for you."

The Chameleon left Barinski to his work and climbed the stone steps to the tower. It was perhaps the most invisible place on earth—this abandoned mosque tucked into a craggy hillside on Despotiko. The Greeks called it "The Goat Island," a barren islet surrounded by a jagged coastline with a goat population that out-numbered the islanders.

Although he owned a number of hideouts, lately the Chameleon had been spending a lot of time at *Minare*—the name he'd given the mosque because of its tall slender tower that jutted high above the abandoned ruins.

When he walked out into the warm island air, he was surprised to see that Melita was already there. Usually she made him wait when he sent for her.

She was gazing out over the water, her long black hair glistening in the sunlight. Like her mother, she had an angel's face and soft vulnerable eyes.

Fiora. He hadn't thought about Melita's mother in years.

"Thinking about jumping to your death?"

She turned, and the pain in her eyes told him she still suffered. That after a year she still hated him for his part in her torment.

"I used to think about it every day when I was first brought here. But no longer. Hello, Father."

"You're looking well. Barinski tells me you've been helping him in the lab. That you have a quick mind and have become useful to him."

"At least I'm useful to someone."

"You could choose to be useful to me. If you agreed to a few simple requests, you could also be free to come and go without—"

"Guards on my heels?"

"They're here to protect you."

"From what, a handful of islanders and their goats?"

As if the goats had been summoned the Chameleon heard their annoying bleating, and he walked to the railing to see a half-dozen shaggy beasts picking the scrubby vegetation along a rocky path that led into the island's treeless interior.

"I grow tired of your constant rebellion, Melita. This misplaced saccharine soul of yours is boring."

"How could Lucifer give birth to anything but evil?"

"You've misinterpreted my motives."

"Then murder and mayhem isn't your passion?"

He faced her. "I prefer to call it revenge."

"Your enemies are not mine."

"They should be. We are more alike than you know. My blood is your blood."

"I'm nothing like you. It's one of the few comforts in my life. How is Simon?"

"Your brother is…resting comfortably."

"Send him my love."

"Of course. Choices, Melita. We all make choices, and must live with the consequences. Simon made his, and you made yours. You may think your punishment has been too harsh, but I demand loyalty and honesty. A year ago you failed at both."

"A price must be paid for our sins. We are in agreement on that, Father. It's what keeps me in constant prayer these days."

"You pray for forgiveness?"

"I pray for justice. That's why I have no intentions of slitting my wrists again, or jumping to my death."

"And this justice you seek… What do you pray for exactly?"

"You killed the only man I will ever love."

"You killed him, Melita. Your betrayal to me killed him."

"The sin you committed that day damned you, as my choice to love Nemo destroyed him and has imprisoned me. What I pray for, Father, is your Armageddon. That it will be swift and final."

Her words should have angered him, but there was fire in her eyes just now, and conviction in her voice. It was the first time he'd heard such determination, and it pleased him beyond words.

Perhaps she was more like him than she knew.

Justice was just another word for revenge. And on that score he understood her passion. The good news was, she no longer wanted to curl up and die.

He would use her craving for *justice* to bring her back to him. And if that didn't work, then perhaps

Barinski would have another guinea pig for his regeneration machine, and he would gain her loyalty without her ever knowing it had been lost.

"I think you deserve a holiday. I'm going home for a few days. I know Callia would love to see you. If you promise to follow the rules, I'll let you come."

"Leave the island?"

"For a few days. Follow the rules and enjoy a taste of freedom."

She hesitated, knowing what that required. He waited, looked past the goats to the coastline while she contemplated the price.

"All right. I'll follow the rules."

The Chameleon refocused on his little Joan of Arc. "Of course you will, Melita, or another poor fool will end up dead, damning your sweet soul to eternal hell. I doubt that you could live through that a second time."

Chapter 1

Six months later

The yacht that had lulled her to sleep hours ago now jerked Allegra Nightingale awake. She sat up just as the yacht's powerful twin engines shut down.

They were stopping.

Why?

She climbed out of bed and looked out the stateroom window. It was early morning and the sun was on the horizon. In the distance she saw a jet boat speeding toward the *Stella di Mare*.

Filip was about to get company.

Yesterday they had cruised through the Strait of Messina and headed up the coast of Italy. Filip hadn't told her where they were going, and she hadn't asked.

He'd been in an unpredictable mood since their exodus from Nescosto.

The attack on the villa had been well-executed, the incursion swift. Nescosto was now a pile of rubble along the Amalfi Coast, and buried beneath it was Filip's brother Yurii.

From the moment Filip had dragged her onto the yacht, she'd known no one else had survived. He'd ordered her below deck, and there she had remained while the *Stella* quickly sped away into the night.

For three days she had danced around him, trying to stay out of his way—feeling as insignificant as a barnacle stealing a ride on the yacht's hull. But now a boat was arriving, and so she pulled on the black sweatpants and gray T-shirt Filip had issued her like a prison uniform on a slave ship.

She left the stateroom, headed through the companionway, and scaled the stairs to the deck. She heard voices and stopped to listen.

"I came as soon as you called."

"You made good time, Lazlo. Is Matyash with you?"

"I'm here, Filip."

Allegra appeared in the morning sunlight just as the man, Matyash, leapt onto the deck from the jet boat christened the *Sera Vedette*. He was a thin man who wore his dark hair long like Filip. His face, however, wasn't nearly as handsome—a long scar cut deep into his cheek and curved into the side of his mouth.

He spied her and sent his eyes on a slow, very deliberate appraisal of her body. The smile that followed puckered his scar and made his appearance grotesque.

"You read my mind, Filip. A little entertainment to pass the days at sea will lighten our moods."

Filip turned.

When his soulless eyes locked with hers, Allegra kept her face as expressionless as his. She had no idea what he would say or do.

Her training had taught her to never show weakness. But today Filip was in control. He had been since they'd fled Nescosto as it crumbled into the sea.

He could let these men take her, and they would use her as unconscionably as they used their guns. And if he chose to pass her from one to another, no amount of protesting would stop them.

If she was entertaining enough perhaps she would survive. If not, she could be tossed overboard.

Chin high, her backbone straight, Allegra waited for the ugly one to make his move, promising herself she would endure whatever ill plan he had for her.

"Leave her be. The woman is mine."

Filip's words were spoken with the same authority that made him such a dangerous adversary to his enemies, and a feeling of relief washed over Allegra.

He held out his hand to her. "Come, Allegra."

He hadn't touched her in three days, but now he wrapped his arm around her waist and pulled her into the protection of his muscular body.

He was a head taller than her five-seven height—an Adonis with wild black hair, high cheekbones and a pair of dark eyes that were as unpredictable as his moods.

Lazlo pulled a piece of paper out of his pocket. Allegra saw that it was a newspaper clipping. Filip dropped his arm from around her and took the paper.

"A little something to fuel the fire inside you," Lazlo said.

Filip scanned the information, and as he did, Allegra craned her neck. It was from an Italian newspaper confirming the death of Yurii and the fall of Nescosto.

The photo was horrifying, the devastation catastrophic. More important the article revealed who had been responsible. The NSA was claiming victory for the insurgence.

Filip crumpled the paper in his hand and tossed it overboard. Allegra moved away from him and went to stand at the railing. Behind her she heard him exchange words with his comrades, and in a matter of minutes the two men returned to the jet boat.

Lazlo spoke to the captain, then followed his friend below. They were back within minutes with duffel bags slung over their shoulders, they boarded the *Stella di Mare* once more.

This time, the man named Lazlo headed into the wheelhouse. The powerful twin engines began to sing, then the luxury yacht quickly moved out.

Allegra remained at the railing, the warm tropical breeze lifting her dark hair around her shoulders as the yacht picked up speed. Yurii was dead, and he'd taken the details of their secret assignment to his grave. She questioned whether Filip was privy to the mission's details. If he was, how long would it be before he shared them with her?

She had no phone. She'd left everything behind when she had fled Nescosto. But if Filip hadn't assured her that they were on the same page by the time they reached land, then she would find a way to contact Cyrus.

She was deep in thought when an explosion rocked the yacht, pitching her into the railing. When she regained her balance and turned around, orange flames and billowing smoke were rising up out of the sea. Filip was holding a detonating device in his hand, and the *Sera Vedette* was gone, as well as its captain.

The death of Yurii Petrov made newspaper headlines across the country. The *Washington Post* must have been lacking news on Wednesday, as they dedicated the entire front page to the incident, and bored the public with a lengthy profile on an international criminal no one was aware existed—no one outside the criminal elite and government intelligence.

The article listed Yurii's many atrocities beginning with money laundering, and ending with his affiliation with the Red Mafia. A color photo of Nescosto, Yurii's headquarters, ate up half the page. If not for the caption, the once sprawling four-story villa built into a sheer rock face along the Amalfi Coast would have been unrecognizable.

The NSA claimed credit for the takedown. They were vague on the details, but that was standard when the special operations group, code-named Onyxx, was involved—they were the invisible spooks no one talked about.

The news story ended with a brief statement from France's Department of Foreign Information and Counterespionage. The SDECE reported that two of their agents had died in the siege.

It was the first Onyxx Agent Ashland Kelly had heard that another intelligence agency was undercover inside Yurii Petrov's citadel at the time he'd planted the explosives, sending Nescosto into the sea. There had been a window of opportunity to escape before detonation—a small window. Had he known about the French agents, their lives could have been spared.

Too bad the left hand hadn't informed the right hand what the hell they were doing. But it was rare to find two agencies willing to share information, let alone work together. The only two who came to mind at the moment were Onyxx and EURO-Quest.

Ash tossed the paper on the couch in his Washington apartment and headed for the shower. When he climbed out, he saw that his boss had left a message on his cell phone. Dripping wet, he tucked the towel around his hips, reached for his phone on the sink, and hit voice mail.

"Did you see the morning paper? Burgess Stillman from the SDECE is on his way to Washington. Before he gets here, we need to talk. My office. As soon as you get this."

Ash headed into his bedroom, dropping the towel in the doorway. He dressed quickly, then left the bedroom wearing jeans, a black V-neck sweater, and his lucky cowboy boots.

On the way to the kitchen, he glanced out the window. It was snowing this morning—big, wet winter flakes that made the November day as gray as his socks. He liked hot weather—desert hot—and he'd never gotten used to the inconvenience of winter, or the dampness that accompanied it.

He made his morning pot of tea, poured a cup to take with him, and grimaced over the fact that there was no time to quell the hunger in his belly.

Thinking about how good a fried egg sandwich would taste, Ash went out the door with his tea, pulling on his brown leather jacket, his shaggy, sandy blonde hair still wet, his jaw unshaven.

The snow wouldn't stay, that was the good news. But it would make the morning commute to headquarters slow. The traffic was already backed up as he pulled his green Jeep out of the underground parking lot, the cars resembling an ant march to a picnic.

He joined the march. As much as he detested crowds and smog, he drove through morning rush hour like a cultured city boy instead of a man used to the hot wind in his face on a dirt road in Mexico.

Ash entered the front doors at Onyxx headquarters forty minutes later. He stepped inside the elevator just as the doors were about to close, and came face-to-face with Burgess Stillman.

He'd never met the SDECE commander, but he'd seen pictures, and heard the rumors about the forty-year-old Frenchman. Six-six, two-sixty, with a silver crewcut, Stillman looked like the kind of guy who ate roadkill for breakfast and asked for seconds.

"Ashland Kelly." Stillman looked him up, then down. "You're thinner than your profile stats, *mon ami*. Merrick must be working your ass off these days."

"Excuse me."

"I don't accept excuses, Kelly. You'll learn that before this is over. I have two dead agents, no bodies to console the families, a superior climbing up my ass, and no way to amputate the hemorrhoid. Not yet."

Ash opened his mouth to defend the mission that had cost the SDECE two agents, then closed it. It had been a straightforward assignment. Get in, get out, and leave nothing standing once Petrov's data had been hijacked, and they'd rescued the female Quest agent, Casmir Balasi.

"You got blood on your hands, *mon ami*. But that's your specialty, isn't it? What is it they call you?" Stillman paused. "*Oui*, I remember. They call you the Ashtray. An appropriate name for a man who likes to play with matches, no?"

Stillman retrieved two pictures from his coat pocket and stuck them in Ash's face. "That's Felton Chanler with his wife, three kids and their dog. This one, Jazmin Grant, was the best damn agent I've had in years. Twenty-eight is too damn young to die."

That was for damn sure, Ash thought staring at the beautiful blonde. "I'm sorry about your agents."

Stillman slid the pictures back in his pocket. "I don't want your condolences, Kelly. I want your hide. But since I won't get away with skinning you alive, I'll settle for my second choice."

"And that would be?"

"You'll know soon enough."

Stillman hit the button on the elevator and it took off. Within minutes they were walking down the corridor side-by-side, headed for Merrick's office.

The SDECE commander knocked, then swung the door open as if he owned the agency and every man in it. He stepped inside the room just as Merrick hung up the phone.

Adolf Merrick arched his gray eyebrows over his chilly blue eyes. "You're early. I didn't expect you until this afternoon."

"I met your firecracker, Merrick. He wouldn't be hard to pick out in a line-up. He fits your MO."

"My MO?"

"*Oui.* Your recruits are a bunch of marauders. Criminals, every last one of them."

"My agents don't have a particular MO, except one, Stillman. They know how to survive. That's what it takes to be successful in this business. Maybe if your agents were made out of similar stuff, they'd still be alive."

"That's a helluva thing for you to say to me."

"Sit down, Ash. Stillman, if you'd like to take a seat down the hall in the waiting room, I'll have a cup of coffee brought to you."

Stillman pulled out the chair in front of Merrick's desk and sat. "I've never taken a number in my life, Merrick, and I don't plan to start now. Your errand boy can wait outside, or stay since he's the reason I'm here."

Ash waited to be dismissed.

Merrick said, "Kelly, take a seat."

Ash made himself comfortable on the couch along the wall. He'd keep his mouth shut. Speak if he was engaged. If not, he'd just take up a little space and oxygen, and enjoy the showdown between Stillman and Merrick. It was going to be entertaining. The temperature in the room was as chilly as the weather outside.

"I've talked with my supervisors about this situation," Merrick began, "and we're sympathetic. No agency likes investing time and money and coming up short. And when agents don't come home, it makes it worse. But that's the business we're in. Sometimes we win big, and sometimes the losses are hard to swallow."

"Save your pat speech. An apology won't fix this, and it's not why I'm here. I want compensation. My number one agent is dead."

"Onyxx is under no obligation to compensate the SDECE. We sympathize," Merrick said again, "but we never make restitutions or apologies. I don't know of any agency that does. We all know the score when we send our men and women into the field."

"You command a gang of fugitives. A well-kept secret that I'm sure the NSA would like to keep hidden in the closet. What do you think the media would do with that kind of information? What do you think the public would say if they knew their tax dollars sanctioned a bunch of criminals?"

Ash said nothing, but he was thinking that for Stillman to know so much about Onyxx, he'd gone digging. All the data on Onyxx and its agents were kept confidential—sealed under lock and key within the Green Room upstairs. No one could access the file without an authorization number. Hell, they couldn't even get through the door without proper ID.

"You mentioned compensation. What is the SDECE proposing?" Merrick asked.

Stillman grinned. "I knew you'd come around, *mon ami*. Adolf Merrick, hotshot assassin for the NSA who doesn't know when to retire and go home, so they hand him a desk job. You're no better than your men. You were once a criminal yourself. Sorry, a survivor."

"We all have a past."

"Baggage in this business can be deadly. You had a beautiful wife once. A pity she died so young and so senselessly. But as you say, that's the business we're in."

Ash winced. Stillman had just crossed the line into forbidden territory. No one at Onyxx talked about Johanna Merrick and her tragic death at the hands of the Chameleon. Merrick's arch enemy was still out there enjoying the fruits of his debauchery, and so far no agency had been able to stop him. He had more hideouts than a centipede had legs.

Merrick leaned back in his chair. "You're a reckless sonofabitch, Stillman. The worst kind of loose cannon. Say what you came to say, then get the hell out of my office."

"You left a loose end in Italy when you pulled out. Yurii Petrov's brother escaped Nescosto before you leveled it."

"We're aware that Filip got away."

"Are you going after him?"

"We know where he's at, and he's being watched."

"A nice way of saying you've learned something that makes him more valuable alive than dead."

Merrick didn't dispute Stillman's claim.

"Unlike you, I don't have the luxury of sitting back and watching. My superiors are demanding answers for the deaths of Chanler and Grant."

"I'm afraid I can't help you with that. Not unless you'd like to tell me what your agents were doing at Nescosto."

"That's classified."

"Even to your superiors?"

"Don't put words in my mouth. The bottom line is your timing at Nescosto couldn't have been worse. Your victory has destroyed any chance for me to get mine. So you can understand why dropping a bomb in the middle of your agency would make me feel marginally better."

Merrick sat back in his chair. "I don't think this has anything to do with the SDECE wanting restitution. I think this is about you, and what you need to save your ass. I'd say your superiors didn't sanction the mission you sent your agents on, and now that they're dead, you're scrambling to salvage a piece of the pie to save your job."

"A colorful scenario, *mon ami*, but untrue. What I came here for was to ask you to—"

"Ask? Let's be clear, Stillman. You came here to muscle me, not *ask*. I can't bring your agents back. As much as I'd like to, I don't have that kind of power."

"But you do have the power to gift the SDECE with a replacement agent. After all, it was your firecracker who killed mine."

Ash had been in the middle of a yawn when Stillman dropped his bomb. He glanced at Merrick and saw that his boss was just as surprised as he was.

Merrick had sacrificed everything for Onyxx—over twenty-five years of his life. His personal happiness. His comrades.

His wife.

His current status was an extension of those sacrifices, and it went far beyond sitting behind a desk in a cushy office.

The bottom line was, he'd earned the right to be whatever he chose to be, which was a supremely confident, fearless commander. He was unflappable and possessive, and some days a real ornery sonofabitch. But Ash had never met a more honest man.

"You want me to hand over one of my men?"

"You're lucky I'm not asking for two. Chanler was a loyal agent, and he will be missed. But Jaz Grant was irreplaceable. Since it was the Ashtray's trigger finger that took her from me, I want him to replace her. An eye for an eye."

"No disrespect to Grant, but Ash is a seasoned veteran. Twice the agent."

"I have files of data that would dispute that, but then I had the privilege of working with Grant for the past six years. She was the most fearless, skillful agent the SDECE has ever recruited. To me the Ashtray is nothing but a criminal who likes to play with fire. Grant was peerless."

"What Ash is, for the record, is the number one explosives expert in the country. Onyxx trained him, and he belongs to me."

"Don't you mean he belongs to Onyxx?"

"I am Onyxx, Stillman. If you've read up on me, then you know that. Contrary to the gossip that continues to question who and what I am, and the one mistake I made sixteen years ago, I still call the shots at this agency. And unlike you, I don't have to check with my superiors every time I blow my nose or scratch my ass."

"Lose one man, or lose your integrity, and the future of Onyxx? You know how it works. How the media loves a good scandal. I guarantee the leak will result in a lengthy investigation. When they're finished the world will know what your men eat for breakfast, how often they piss, and every dirty secret you've covered up to bring them into this agency."

"You're blackmailing me?"

"I'm sure you've done worse to get what you want. One man to replace the two he killed. That's my deal. It's a small price to keep Onyxx the NSA's best kept secret, don't you think?"

"And you plan to send one agent after Filip Petrov."

"What I plan to do with him is no concern of yours once he's mine, *mon ami*."

"My answer is no. I won't hand him over so you can send him on some suicide mission."

"You don't sound like you have much faith in your man. As you said, he's no ordinary agent. He's a survivor."

"You have my answer."

"Then this is the end of Onyxx, Merrick. I promise you I won't rest until I've exposed you, and every man in this agency."

Ash expected his boss to counter Stillman's threat with one of his own, or maybe offer a more reasonable solution. But Merrick only watched as the Frenchman stood and headed for the door.

Ash sat forward and cleared his throat.

Merrick looked at him, shook his head—a warning to keep his mouth shut. But how could he do that? They were about to be crucified by the media. Onyxx would be flushed down the toilet, along with every man with a checkered past. And that would be Merrick's entire team of rat fighters—his team.

"I'll do it," he said.

"The hell you will." Merrick's fist crashed down on his desk. "I won't agree to it."

"I can opt out of my contract," Ash reminded. "I've put in my seven years. I'm a free agent if I want to be. I can leave any time."

"We'll discuss it later."

"It won't change anything." Ash stood and faced Stillman. "I'll be your dog under one condition."

"You're in no position to make demands, Kelly."

"If you want me, then put in writing that the SDECE doesn't hold Onyxx responsible for the deaths of their two agents, and they have no plans to undermine Onyxx in the future in any way. Once Merrick receives the document and approves it, I'll be on the next plane to France."

Stillman grinned. "Your trigger boy is smarter than he looks. Or should I say, my trigger boy. The paperwork will be on your desk in two days. *Au revoir,* Merrick." He turned to Ash. "Welcome to the SDECE, Mr. Kelly. *À bientôt.*"

Two days later, with a crust of snow still blanketing the ground, and a gray sky threatening more of the white stuff by noon, Ash arrived at Onyxx and went straight to Merrick's office. When he stepped through the door he saw his boss studying a document on his desk.

Burgess Stillman hadn't wasted any time. It looked like he should start packing for Paris.

He wasn't happy about that, but if it guaranteed that Onyxx wouldn't be exploited, he'd make the sacrifice. He owed Merrick more than just his life.

"Have a seat, Ash. I'm sure you know why I called you in."

"How does it read? Will it keep Onyxx out of the hot seat?"

"It will." Merrick leaned back in his chair and folded

his arms over his chest. "We could refuse the letter and let whatever happens happen."

Ash sat. "Call Stillman's bluff? I don't think so. My take on him is that he doesn't make idle threats. Besides, Onyxx can live without me. One man doesn't make an agency."

"You hated what Onyxx stood for when I brought you in. Now you act as though you actually like us here."

"I didn't have a choice back then. But today I know it was the best thing that could have ever happened to me and my family."

"I needed you back then, and the agency still needs you today. Contrary to what you think, you won't be easy to replace."

Ash grinned. "You'll find another criminal in a tight spot. Someone who wants a second chance."

"I told Stillman it takes an outlaw's mentality to survive in this business, but it takes a helluva lot more than that. It takes a man who values loyalty and is willing to bet his last breath on himself and his comrades. It's true my men have traveled both sides of the line, but that's just a small part of who they are."

Merrick steepled his fingers on his chest. "I know why you did this. You blame yourself for the deaths of those two French agents, just like you still blame yourself for Sully's death in Greece. But you can't fix this any more than you can bring those agents back, or Sully."

"I won't pretend that it doesn't bother me that Stillman's agents are dead. Or that one was a woman, and that it was my bomb that killed her. Had we known they were there, they could have gotten out in time."

"I don't want you going into this feeling guilty. Guilt eats at a man, and it can make him take chances he wouldn't normally take. So don't make this personal."

Merrick chastising him for living with guilt—that was choice, coming from a man, who after seventeen years, continued to carry around an acre of blame over his wife's death.

They were more alike than anyone knew, perhaps more than any of the other rat fighters. They were both recovering alcoholics, both had lost family and close friends, and both felt responsible for their deaths.

Guilt, the blood-sucking parasite that no amount of therapy or alcohol could suffocate.

"As callous as this is going to sound, we deal in casualties every day here. On the other hand, I don't want you becoming one more statistic for the SDECE. Use everything you've learned to stay alive. It could take some time, but I'll find a way to get you out from under Stillman's thumb. Only a handful of people know who you really are. Your survival in that stink hole prison in Chihuahua gives you an edge. Anything Stillman throws at you I know you can survive."

"Then don't worry about me."

"I'm not worried, I'm pissed off."

"You have a right to be. Stillman is an unlikable sonofabitch."

"On a lighter note, did you get to see your family while you were on sabbatical?"

"Yes. I spent a few weeks in Mexico, then bought a

boat and sailed to Spain. It was good to see my mother. She seems happy. Robena, too. My little sister is getting married in a few months."

"And your cousin?"

"Naldo… He's not doing as good as I'd hoped. He misses the old life. Probably always will."

"Do you miss it?"

Ash shrugged. "Not so much. We were rebels back then, me and Naldo. Horny bastards with no limits, and too much money to value what was really important. I see things differently now."

"I'll contact Stillman and let him know you'll be in Paris tomorrow. Watch your back and don't trust anyone. Stillman's a desperate man, and desperate men play desperate games."

"A desert scorpion doesn't curl up and die when he's cornered." Ash grinned. "He just gets meaner."

Merrick's serious expression softened and a hint of a smile tickled his gray mustache. "Use the past, and whatever else you've learned here at Onyxx to keep breathing. And if you need anything, call. Stillman might believe you're his new trigger boy, but you're just on loan."

Ash stood and extended his hand. "You're a straight shooter, Merrick. I've always respected that. Whatever happens, know that I'm grateful for what you did for me and my family."

Chapter 2

"The men in this screwed-up world are always going to run it, baby doll. No sense fighting what you can't change. But a woman can survive if she can cash in on a man's weaknesses. He's got two, his belly and what dangles between his legs. So learn how to cook, and how to ride a man with confidence. Take it from your mama, the bills don't get paid going to church and keeping your legs crossed. That was a joke, baby doll. Crossed...get it?"

A smile surfaced on Allegra's face. For months she had been struggling to remember pieces of the past. But Bonnie had never left her.

Her mother had found a way to survive in a world that had dealt her a going-broke hand. Allegra had been six when her father had left them. He was a selfish man who never should have had a family.

The bitter truth had turned Bonnie against men, but it hadn't stopped her from using them to pay the bills. When Allegra turned sixteen, a fancy-dressed lawyer paid her a visit the morning after her mother died. It was then she had come to realize just how much her mother had sacrificed—Mama's will allowed her to be buried in style, with enough left over for Allegra to go to college.

The trip up the coast had all been about Bonnie's wisdom. Allegra had been conditioned to survive. It had been how she'd lived all her life.

That's why she'd seen to the cooking over the past four days and focused on Filip's belly. What dangled between his legs, however, hadn't been addressed yet. Filip had made no attempt to touch *his woman*. He hadn't taken her to his bed, or come to hers.

Although she would have been as flawless and efficient in bed as she was in the kitchen—thanks to Bonnie's education—Allegra felt relieved that she hadn't been put to that test. Not yet anyway.

The morning of the fifth day they reached Zadar on the coast of Croatia. They had sailed into port before noon, and immediately come ashore. Filip took her shopping to buy her a coat—he said it was snowing in Budapest.

It was the first time he'd mentioned where they were going.

By late afternoon they'd arrived at a secluded airstrip, and minutes later they had boarded a plane and it had taken off.

"If anyone asks who you are, you will tell them you're my woman."

Filip had left Lazlo and Matyash to come and sit

next to her. Allegra had been staring out the window. She turned to look at him. "Am I your woman?"

"I have no need for a woman."

"Then why are we playing this game?"

"You don't want my protection?"

"I'd just like to know why you're giving it."

"Call it a gift."

"You're not known to be a gift giver."

"A woman who speaks her mind, and is not afraid of me…" His eyes searched hers. "It's been a long time since I've been in the company of such a strong woman. No wonder he chose you."

"You know?"

"Why you were at Nescosto? Of course."

"Can you tell me? Yurii never shared details. He said I'd know the extent of the mission when the time came."

"There is no reason to alter that. For now you are my woman. That is the only game you need to concentrate on."

He pulled a gun from his pocket and handed it to her and Allegra took it. The small-caliber Beretta Tomcat wasn't a favorite of hers, but right now having a weapon of any kind made her feel better.

She slipped it in her coat pocket as he leaned close and whispered, "I'm told that you can hit anything you aim at. Even wearing a blindfold in a blackout. But that's just one of your talents. Cyrus says he's never seen a woman as resilient as you."

"You clean up well, Mr. Kelly. You no longer look like an alley rat living in the bottom of a Dumpster."

Ash let the comment roll off his back. A haircut and

new clothes didn't change a man, but he was curious as to why it had been on the top of Stillman's list once he'd arrived in Paris.

He'd flown in yesterday afternoon, and as he'd entered Stillman's office at the SDECE, the man had been wearing a grin as wide as the Atlantic. Stillman had given him a list of errands to attend to before morning—a haircut and new clothes. A facial and manicure—he'd never had either in his life.

He relaxed into the backseat next to Stillman as their driver changed lanes and picked up speed.

"For this mission you're going to have to return to your old life, Mr. Kelly. Or should I say, Señor Toriago?"

Toriago...

Sonofabitch. Stillman knew his true identity.

Ash refused to let the sick feeling in his gut surface on his face. A weaker man would have surrendered to the noose that had just been placed around his neck, but a weak man was a dead man. He wasn't afraid to die— had never been afraid—but Stillman's announcement threatened something more precious than his own life. If he knew Ash Kelly was Marco Toriago, then there was a good chance he also knew the truth about his family.

He said, "Ash Kelly agreed to work for the SDECE. Not Marco Toriago. He died eight years ago."

"Yes, I know how the story goes. You died in a Mexican prison along with your father. We both know that fabrication was the handiwork of Adolf Merrick. The legacy your father left behind is ready to be reborn, and with it, you, twice as disreputable as you were in the old days. At the moment I have no need for the

Ashtray, but I do have need for his notorious counterpart."

"This isn't what I agreed to."

"You agreed to work for me in whatever capacity I require. You agreed to that to save Onyxx. A loyal gesture. Does that mean Marco Toriago has grown a conscience?"

"I said, he's dead."

"I hope not, for your sake and your family's. I am curious how Merrick managed it, though. The head of a famous drug cartel's son turned special agent. What did he promise you? Refuge for your family? New identities? Freedom and a happy ending for all if you sold your soul to him?"

"My family isn't a part of this."

Ash had meant to keep his voice even, but he'd failed, and like the snake he was, Stillman struck quickly.

"On the contrary, I'd say that your family has been the driving force behind everything you've done since Merrick pulled you out of that ghetto prison. Now then, let's get down to business. Your plane leaves within the hour for Budapest."

"What's in Budapest?"

"It's where an important delivery is about to take place. One you are going to intercept. The courier is Filip Petrov, and Casso Salavich is his destination. I'm sure you've heard of him. He's an untouchable who has his fingers in more dirty deals than we can count."

Ash knew who he was. "And what will I be intercepting?"

"A top secret disk was stolen from the SDECE. For security reasons, the disk was treated with an acid solution that would scramble it in twenty-four hours if it was exposed to air. It was also encrypted. I'm not sure if you'll be looking for another disk, or if it will be a hard copy."

"Is there a chance the acid wiped out the disk before the data was stripped?"

"I don't think that happened."

"Why?"

"Because Filip is on his way to Salavich, who is a master decoder. Filip wouldn't be here if he wasn't carrying the information on him. He has it, some form of it, and within days it's about to be decoded."

"What's on it?"

"The SDECE's security codes. All of them. Your job is to recover it before it's decoded."

"From Casso Salavich."

Stillman smiled. "Normally that would be difficult, getting close to a man who never leaves his house without an army of bodyguards, but the good news is, he's being challenged by a number of his enemies who would like to take control of his drug trafficking operation. As you well know, the demand to stay on top in the drug business is a heavy burden. At present he is looking for more power, and a way to prove himself kingpin."

Ash listened, knowing where this was headed.

"You're going to be his salvation and lift his burden by going into business with him. At least it will appear that way, a viable cover for you to infiltrate his operation and recover the stolen data when it arrives."

"That's it? Recover the data?"

"Not quite. There's still the matter of who stole the disk."

"Do you know?"

"*Oui*. At the time I wasn't aware of it, but there was a traitor among us at the SDECE." Stillman released a heavy sigh. "I have reason to believe it was Jazmin Grant."

"Then your problem is solved. Grant died at Nescosto."

"There's no proof of that. Just because you blew Nescosto sky high doesn't mean everyone died. Filip Petrov managed to survive."

"And Chanler?"

"Chanler is dead. But Grant… She's the best agent I've ever worked with. That's why she was able to fool me."

"I'm an explosives expert, not an assassin."

"I don't want her dead. I want her brought back to me alive. I want to know why she betrayed me. She's the only one who can answer that."

"Why the game? Why didn't you just come clean with Merrick? We could have worked together on this."

"And have it on record that the SDECE has been negligent, and that one of their own is a traitor?"

"Were you negligent?"

"My only fault was trusting Grant's reputation, her years of loyalty, and giving her a second chance when I should have buried her."

"A second chance?"

"The past doesn't affect your mission. Recover the data and then find Grant."

"And where will I find her?"

"If I knew that, I would already have her in chains." Stillman handed Ash a sophisticated cell phone. "I'm sure you're familiar with one of these. Everything you need to know about Salavich and Grant can be accessed in the database. You can also find my private number in there under my code name, Artus. And here's a watch with a sophisticated explosive device you might need should you find yourself in a tight spot."

"If I'm back in the drug business I'll need merchandise."

"Tell Salavich you have a billion dollars worth of premium ice to sell for starters. Give him some bull about scheduled monthly deliveries. You're the expert on that, so it'll be your job to entice him into your deception. I'm confident you'll save the SDECE before it's compromised, and before you have to deliver on your promise to Salavich."

"I've been out of the drug business for eight years. Don't you think Salavich is going to be suspicious?"

"Your job is to convince him otherwise. If Merrick hadn't come along when he did, you would have finished out your sentence in that Mexican hellhole, then gone back into business. Big business. The Toriagos never did anything small."

"But he did come along, and I didn't go back."

"And now that makes you a man of respectability?" Stillman snorted. "I have a list of your atrocities, so don't pretend that you're a changed man. We never shed our old skin completely, Toriago, and your status at Onyxx proves that. You're a drug-dealing ex-con who traded one prison for another when you agreed to become one of Merrick's elite marauders. This mission isn't any different from those you've done for Onyxx, except that you have a new jailer. Me."

"You overestimate my talent, Stillman."

"Perhaps you underestimate it. You're Estabon Toriago's son. The most ruthless drug lord in Mexico, ever. Like father, like son?" Stillman glanced down at Ash's feet. "I thought I told you to get rid of those old boots. You're trying to impress a billionaire."

"My boots stay, Stillman. It's the one part of Marco Toriago that never died."

"Let's hope there is more left of Toriago than a pair of worn-out cowboy boots. You've been given a limitless bank account. Dress the part and convince Salavich that money is what drives you. Convince him you're back in business. Big business."

"And if Salavich doesn't bite?"

"He'll be wary at first, but an alliance with Estabon Toriago's son…" Stillman's grin was back. "Even the most cautious criminal wouldn't be able to resist going into business with the son of a legend."

"And if Salavich decides to kill me instead?"

"Then I'll concede I was mistaken about you, and I'll send my regards to your family."

The car sped into the parking lot at the Paris airport. Ash got out and Stillman followed. The driver popped the trunk and Ash grabbed his one piece of luggage.

"I've seen to everything you'll need. Passport. Money. Credit cards. You have a suite at the Corinthia Grand Hotel Royal in Budapest. Good luck." Stillman patted Ash on the back. "You're once again in the drug business, Mr. Toriago. Let's hope, for your family's sake, you still remember how to play the game."

An hour later Ash found his seat on the plane in first class. Before the flight took off he located the minitransmitter inside the cell phone. He dropped the pill-size electronic bug on the floor and crushed it beneath the heel of his boot, then found the one in the watch.

So much for Stillman keeping track of him. He intended to see the mission through, but without his *jailer* tracking his ass.

He skimmed the file on Salavich, then moved on to Jazmin Grant's profile. He studied the photo, read her stats. Stillman's blond beauty was five-seven, weighed one-twenty-five, had brown eyes, a nice rack and great legs—she could have made a fortune as a stripper.

The striking blonde reminded Ash of the old days. If he'd seen her in a bar in Mexico, Marco Toriago would have definitely singled her out of the crowd and paid any amount of money to get her naked.

But it had been years since he'd played hard and partied even harder. He wasn't kidding when he had told Stillman that Marco Toriago had died in prison eight years ago. He wasn't the same man, but somehow he was going to have to resurrect the dead to play this game and win.

On the flight Ash brushed up on his Spanish, and four hours later Marco Toriago exited the plane in Budapest and made two phone calls. The first one went to Casso Salavich to make an appointment to discuss a business proposition. Prepared to be put off, he was surprised when Salavich invited Estabon Toriago's son to his bastion on the Danube for drinks at four o'clock the next day.

The second call he made to Girona, Spain. After talking to his mother and learning all was well, he asked to speak to his cousin.

Naldo was anxious for a change in scenery, so he invited him to Budapest.

Chapter 3

The first shot shattered the windshield and took out the driver. Lazlo slumped forward, and before his forehead hit the steering wheel he was dead.

A second shot sailed through the broken windshield seconds later. It snapped Matyash's head back as the bullet took a chunk out of his cheek, spraying his warm blood on the roof of the car and into the backseat where Allegra sat next to Filip.

The shots were followed by a volley of gunfire that rocked the silver BMW and shattered more windows.

The car shook as it continued to be riddled with more artillery. Allegra screamed and ducked low into the seat. She heard Filip swear in Italian, felt his hand on her shoulder shoving her farther onto the floor. Then he opened the rear car door.

"Filip, wait! You can't go out there."

"Stay down."

Filip rolled out of the car onto the ground and into the fresh snow that had fallen overnight, then got up and started to run.

More shots rang out, but the car was no longer the target. The reprieve gave Allegra time to pull the Beretta from her pocket. She raised up from the floor and surveyed her surroundings. Filip was halfway to a grove of trees dodging bullets as they rained down around him.

Across the river she spotted a flash of light. It had to be the shooter. The target was too far for her to do any damage with a handgun so she didn't waste the ammo.

The gunfire stopped as soon as Filip disappeared into the trees. But the reprieve didn't last long before the gunman began to unload a pound of lead into the car again shattering the side windows. She heard Matyash groan and gasp from the front seat. He must have taken another hit. Maybe more than one.

She heard Filip yell from the trees, ordering her to get out of the car. While she was weighing her decision on how to do that without being cut down, the sound of squealing tires entered the chaos. Through the open door, Allegra saw a black limo pull up beside the car. The back door swung open and a heavy male voice inside ordered her to get in.

"Move, or die!"

Allegra hesitated only a split second before she scrambled off the floor and dove into the backseat of the limousine. As soon as she was inside, the black stretch raced backward, the back door still hanging open. The unexpected speed pitched her into the stranger's lap. She heard him grunt, felt his hands wrap around her waist. He pulled her into the seat beside him and pushed her head into his lap.

"Stay there, *señorita.*"

Her head was spinning as the car continued to speed backward.

"*Pararse*, Naldo," the stranger ordered, and the car immediately came to a screeching stop. Allegra jerked her head up to see what was going on. Through the tinted window she saw Filip break away from the trees and sprint toward the car in an effort to catch a ride. Dodging an onslaught of bullets he dove inside.

Once Filip was seated, the stranger ordered his driver to get them out of there.

As if the chauffeur was once a race car pro, the long stretch whipped around and sped away from the gate like it had grown a pair of wings. Seconds later an explosion shook the limo, and Allegra looked back to see that the car stalled at the gate entrance to Casso Salavich's bastion was engulfed in flames.

"Where to, Señor Toriago?" the chauffeur asked.

"Back to the hotel. *Dese prisa.*"

The limo picked up speed.

Allegra had just started to relax when Filip pulled a 9 mm SIG from his pocket and aimed it at their savior. Just as quickly, the stranger pulled a Spanish Astra with similar lines to the Sig, and curled his arm around her, poking the weapon into her ribs.

"You have lost much today, *señor*. Do you wish to lose more?"

"If you shoot her, I shoot you."

"Where I come from, that is called a Mexican standoff. A situation such as this usually ends up with someone getting anxious and making a hasty decision. In the end no one wins."

"What do you want?" Filip demanded.

"A little gratitude, perhaps. You are still breathing, no?"

"For how long?"

"That is up to you. I have no wish to kill you, *señor*. That was the shooter's agenda, the one hiding on the other side of the river."

"Your driver called you Toriago. That name is familiar. An old name dead and gone."

"It is an old name, *sì*, but I am not dead. And who would you be?"

"Filip Petrov."

"Petrov… I recently read something in the paper about the Petrov family. You've had a string of bad luck lately. A pity to lose the pretty woman, too."

"I have only your word that you didn't hire that shooter."

"You have nothing I want. Almost nothing." Suddenly the stranger pulled Allegra closer to him. "Where I come from, when a man saves another man's life, he is rewarded with a gift." He angled his head and boldly inhaled Allegra's scent like an animal sniffing fresh meat. "You are a lucky man, Petrov. I wish to be so lucky."

"I'm afraid I can't accommodate you, Mr. Toriago. The woman is mine."

"If she was mine, I would not give her up either."

His voice was deep, his Spanish accent as charismatic as his clear blue eyes and killer grin.

He was a combination of contradictions. Pale brown hair, streaked with sunbaked highlights, olive skin, and an American flare for boldness and nice clothes.

A man of mixed worlds.

Filip said, "Toriago… The Toriago cartel from Mexico?"

"*Sì*, from Mexico."

"Your family was also in the newspaper." Filip lowered his gun. "It was a few years ago, but I remember it well. Estabon Toriago and his son died in a Mexican prison. Who are you, the cousin who escaped on his belly like a snake in the grass?"

Suddenly the car sped up, taking on renewed speed. A reckless suicide speed.

Toriago pulled his gun away from Allegra's side and laid it on the seat next to him. "There are no cowards in the Toriago family. We also believe that a good rumor is priceless."

"Meaning?"

"Estabon's son did not die. Not unless I'm a ghost."

"You're Marco Toriago?"

"The very one, *señor*. How bad were you hit?"

Hit? Allegra glanced at Filip, and there, inside his leather jacket, she saw his bloody shirt.

"Filip!"

"Shut up."

The minute Toriago loosened his hold on her, Allegra scrambled across the seat to sit next to Filip. He looked dreadfully pale—why she hadn't noticed that before she couldn't say. She tried to take a closer look at his wound, but he shoved her away.

"Later."

"There's so much blood, Filip. You need a doctor."

"No doctor."

"But—"

"No doctor."

"We have to stop the bleeding."

"I've lived through worse."

"It looks like Señor Salavich doesn't like you much," Toriago said.

"It wasn't Salavich who ambushed me."

The stranger leaned forward and took one end of Filip's jacket and opened it. "The *señorita* is right. You're in bad shape. I can stop the bleeding. That's if you're not afraid of a bit more pain and a little fire."

Toriago grinned. The grin suggested that he was joking, but his cool demeanor, and the worldly experience he exuded, promised otherwise.

"It's the quickest way I know to cauterize a wound when a man is on the run and wants to wake up tomorrow. Of course, it's your call."

"Is this experience talking?" Filip asked.

"I'm not a man who puts much truth in rumors. A man who lives in our world shouldn't." He shrugged. "You might be able to survive. That depends on you. Who can say, Señor Petrov? Life is a gamble, no?"

"Show me."

"Show you what?"

"Bullet holes and fire leave scars. You should have both if you're a man who deals in truth instead of rumors."

Toriago hesitated a moment before slipping off his brown leather jacket. He unbuttoned his white shirt, pulling it from his jeans to expose hard muscles and a bronze six pack. Unfastening his belt one handed—as if he'd done it a thousand times in a dark alley on a minute's notice—he unzipped his pants.

Allegra didn't look away, even when he rolled his right hip forward and jerked his pants low to expose a hideous scar just below his hip bone—a bullet wound that had been cauterized by fire.

His eyes shifted from Filip to her, then back again. "As I said, rumors are for weak men who enter the fight after the smoke has settled."

Allegra studied the puckered wound—a wound that should have killed him. His pants rode low, another inch and it would expose the rest of his perfection. And it would be perfect. A man like him would have the complete package.

Her attention drifted. Any woman would have done the same. The smattering of hair on his chest continued past his deep-set navel and headed south—a narrow strip disappearing into his pants.

She glanced up, saw that his eyes were once again on her. His grin turned rogue, and they shared a moment. He hadn't only caught her in the act of staring, but he'd read her mind as well.

The awkward moment was broken by Filip. "Do it."

Do it? Allegra jerked her head toward Filip. He had to be insane if he was going to let Toriago set him on fire. She was about to tell him as much, then thought better of it.

She kept quite while Toriago zipped his pants, then

reached for a box tucked in a compact cupboard built into the limo's console.

"Take off your coat."

Filip tried, but in the end Allegra had to assist him.

Toriago took something from the box, then a cigarette lighter from his jacket pocket. "Get rid of your shirt, too."

Allegra unbuttoned Filip's bloody shirt, and as she helped him out of it, she saw that the bullet had passed through him high on his chest—a chest that was covered with old scars, souvenirs that branded him as much of a survivor as Toriago.

Toriago sat forward and that's when she saw the disks that resembled lemon drops. She recognized them for what they were. The question was, where had he gotten state-of-the-art explosives?

"Tell your woman to come back and sit by me. You're going to turn into a wild animal in a minute. After that, if you're lucky, you'll pass out."

"I won't pass out," Filip insisted.

"You should hope that you do. Tell her."

Filip glanced at Allegra. "Do what he says."

She hesitated, then slid across the seat.

"Take a deep breath, *señor,* and let it out slowly."

One minute Filip was inhaling air, and the next minute Toriago was on the edge of his seat inserting the candy into Filip's wound. A second later he flicked his lighter to life and said, "Fire in the hole."

When the flame touched the small charge of explosives there was a popping noise and then flames were scorching Filip's chest, cauterizing the wound.

Filip twisted in pain, moaned like a dying animal.

The stench of burnt flesh filled the inside of the car and immediately Allegra felt sick to her stomach. When Filip wrenched forward and began to convulse, Toriago grabbed him by the back of the neck and held him down while he inserted the second disk into the exit wound, then touched it with his lighter once again.

More moaning filled the inside of the limo, more of Filip convulsing in endless pain.

Then he passed out.

Allegra's stomach rolled. She turned to look out the window, the air so putrid and caustic she could taste it in the back of her throat. She didn't look back for several minutes, but when she did Toriago had laid Filip flat and tossed his jacket over him.

She glanced at Toriago who was now reclining in his seat. He pulled a cigarette from his shirt pocket and lit it with his lighter. He seemed unaffected by what he'd done, unaffected by the lingering stench inside the limo.

He began to button his shirt, and as he did, he glanced at her. "Smoke, *señorita?*"

"No."

"If you're going to be sick, let me know. Naldo will pull over."

She shook her head, swallowed the bile rising in her throat. "Will he be all right?"

"The odds are better than they were a few minutes ago. Now then, *señorita*. Tell me why a pretty face, with a body made for love, is with a man who knows nothing about what a woman wants or needs?"

"That would be my business."

"Bad business decisions can be deadly. You should rethink this one."

She didn't answer. She slid as far as she could toward the window and looked out at the passing scenery as they followed the river back into Budapest.

"Don't worry, *señorita*. If he dies, I will see that you don't go hungry. If your body is as beautiful as your face, I'm sure I can find a use for you."

He seemed to take great pleasure in baiting her. Let him, she thought. Let him think she was nothing more than a silly woman to be used by the men in this crazy world. Bonnie had taught her different, a way to survive no matter the cost.

Filip never regained consciousness the entire drive into the city. Allegra continued to stare out the window while Toriago smoked.

Finally he said, "It's going to be important that you keep him immobile for at least twenty-four hours. I've got a suite at the Grand Royal with an extra bedroom. You're welcome to it."

With Filip passed out, Allegra was forced to make a decision. Not sure what to do, she debated on what Filip would want.

Toriago must have read her indecision. "My driver can drop you wherever you wish, *señorita*. Perhaps Filip has a friend you can call."

The only friends Filip had were dead, left behind in a burning car. Filip hadn't explained why they were headed to Casso Salavich's bastion, and going back there seemed reckless at the moment. Maybe Toriago was right. Maybe Salavich was responsible for the attack on their car.

He raised his hand and brushed a strand of her dark hair away from her cheek, tucked it behind her ear. "You should let me treat that cut on your cheek."

It was the first she realized that she'd been injured. She touched her cheek, and came away with blood on her fingers.

"I think gunpowder and a little fire…in the hole is extreme in my case. I'll pass on your offer."

"A woman with a sense of humor. I like that." He was grinning again. "I have something in my room that will prevent a scar. Interested?"

"I'm not worried about a little scar."

"But why live with one if you don't have to?"

His phone rang, and he reached into his pocket for his cell. Flipping it open, he said, "Toriago, here. You're the man with the iron fortress, you should have that answer, not me. I'd say one shooter by the timing of the rounds. Across the river. No. I'll pass today. If you can prove that the shooter was an outside interference, I'll reschedule our appointment. If not, I'll find someone else to sell my merchandise to."

Allegra listened to every word of the one-sided conversation. It had to be Salavich on the phone.

When Toriago disconnected he confirmed her suspicion. He said, "Salavich wants me to return to Ballvaro. He says his men are out searching for the shooter. If you want, my driver will take you and Petrov back once he drops me at my hotel."

Allegra thought a moment, then shook her head. "I think you're right. I'd like to know who blew up our car, and why, before I get trapped behind Ballvaro's iron gate."

Toriago's piercing blue eyes went on a slow, thorough shakedown of her body. "So there's more to you than just a pretty face, and a sense of humor. This is good to know, *señorita*."

* * *

When Naldo pulled the limo up in front of the Grand Royal, Ash handed the dark-haired *señorita* his suite key. "I'll be there shortly."

"With Filip?"

"That was the plan. Unless you're anxious to be alone with me. In that case I'll stash him in the trunk for a couple of hours."

"You've picked an odd time to make a joke."

"It was no joke."

She pulled the Beretta from her pocket and leveled it at his chest. Ash had guessed right. She'd had her hand in her pocket the entire way into town.

"So, *señorita*, you have appeased my curiosity. Do you know how to use it?"

"*Sì*," she mimicked, "and without the slightest hesitation."

She had a sweet brown mole at the corner of her full upper lip, a sexy French accent, and flashy green eyes. She reminded Ash of the old days. As Marco Toriago, he would have had her undressed by now and halfway to nirvana, even if there had been an audience—unconscious or not. Back in Mexico, Toriago had had an unquenchable thirst for ten-minute sex.

The beauty seated beside him deserved more than ten minutes, however. The question was, if he had time and she was willing, could he get it up? For the past year he'd had a problem. It was like his body had simply gone on strike. Too much liquor and guilt, the shrink had said.

"How are you going to get Filip up to the room?"

Her question brought him back. "You let me worry about your boyfriend. I'll figure something out. I always do." He offered her his best killer smile, the one Toriago would have used in Mexico to get her into the back alley. "Now why don't you put your toy away and head up to my room?"

"I promise you that if Filip isn't with you when you show up, I won't think twice about firing my toy at your head."

"It doesn't make much sense for me to go to the trouble of keeping Petrov alive, only to kill him a half hour later. Now, I never repeat myself, but I'm making an exception this once because you've had bad day. Put the gun away, *señorita*."

Her nostrils flared, and she parted her lips as if she had more to say. She was a strong woman, but then she would have to be to survive in Filip Petrov's world. The question was, why would she want to?

She waited too long. Challenging him was a mistake, but she had done it and now he would have to make good on his threat.

He gripped her knee with his right hand, and his bold trespass startled her. She immediately dropped her gaze. A normal reaction, but the wrong one in this case. He knocked the gun from her hand and forced her back against the seat. Curling his body inward, his face inches from hers, his fingers moved farther into the warm space between her thighs. He said, "I'm a man of my word, *señorita*. Something to remember."

To drive the point home, he slid his hand upward, trespassing further, his fingers moving over the front of her pants.

Her heart was pounding, her eyes wide, but she didn't lose her composure. "What now, Toriago?"

He released her and picked the gun up off the floor and gave it back to her. "Now we start over." He offered her his key. "Room 811."

She took the key, then glanced at Filip. She touched his neck, searching for a pulse. When she found it she said, "Make sure he's still breathing when you bring him up."

"Or you're going to take my head off."

She pocketed her gun. "You surprised me once. It won't happen again." Then she swung the door open and exited the limo.

A blast of crisp air joined Ash in the back seat as he watched her walk away and disappear inside.

"You done looking and licking your chops?"

Ash turned to see Naldo eyeing him from the front seat.

"*Sì*, I'm done." Ash pulled the door shut. "Find the cargo entrance."

"You're lucky you're my favorite cousin. You never mentioned I would be dodging bullets on this caper."

"I'm your only cousin. Don't pretend you didn't enjoy yourself."

"*Sì*, it's true." Naldo was grinning, but when he glanced down at Filip Petrov it was gone. "I should cut that bastard's tongue out. I am no coward."

"Forget him."

Naldo nodded. Then added, "For now."

Ash and his cousin were the same age. Just over thirty, they had been as close as brothers. Naldo's parents had been killed in a car accident, and he had come to live with Estabon at age six. They had shared the same bedroom, girlfriends, and when they were older, their passion for excess in all things.

When Ash had called Girona, he hadn't intended to ask his cousin to join him, but the truth was, there was no one better to watch his back in Budapest.

Naldo removed the chauffeur's hat and his jet black, straight hair fell around his face. The one obvious difference that had set them apart was his cousin's prominent Spanish-Portuguese heritage.

Estabon had gone against tradition and married an American beauty with blond hair and blue eyes. Ash's mother had struggled for acceptance in the Toriago family, and she had passed that same struggle on to her blond-haired, blue-eyed son. Robena had been luckier. She looked more like Naldo's sister than his.

"They must pay you well to put up with assholes like that one. In Mexico we would have cut his tongue out."

Ash nodded. "*Sì,* we would have, but we played by different rules back then."

"We played by no rules, *primo.*" Naldo flashed a grin. "What do you think of the shower?"

"What?"

"The shower in my room was made for a party. I could fit six women inside at one time. How about we have a party? Celebrate the old days."

Ash laughed. "Too bad you don't know six women."

"I've only been here a day. There is time. Remember when we used to play stack the deck?"

"We were a lot younger."

"Vigorous bulls, *sì.* But in such a hurry. We are wiser now, no? I'm told Hungarian women like experienced men who take their time."

They found the cargo entrance, and Ash instructed Naldo to park the limo in the underground loading zone. Before he stepped out of the car, he said, "Give me your coat and hat."

Minutes later, wearing the chauffeur's uniform, Ash entered the delivery entrance. He located the laundry room, took an empty cart and tossed in two dozen towels. Acting like just another delivery worker, he wheeled the cart out to the loading zone and headed for the limo.

With Naldo's help, he loaded Petrov into the cart, then covered him up with the towels. Before he wheeled Filip back inside, he said to Naldo, "I shouldn't need you the rest of the day, but stay close."

"I'll be in the bar." Naldo ran his hand through his shaggy hair. "If I can round up that party, want me to give you a call? Or are you going to be too busy with the pretty *señorita?*"

"You noticed."

"Of course. You did, too. I saw the way you were looking at her. Maybe you can bring her to the party. You don't use it, you lose it."

Ain't it the truth, Ash thought. He would party with Naldo after he got Stillman off his back—that's if he could convince his body to go off strike. But right now he needed to stay focused on the job—he had no idea how much time he had to recover the disk.

He pulled the chauffeur's hat down to shield his eyes, then with Filip hidden under the towels, he wheeled Petrov into the hotel.

Chapter 4

In the intelligence business a set of bull-size balls was an advantage, not a handicap. So it wasn't Stillman's arrogance that had pissed off Merrick.

Loyalty was an admirable trait, if that was what had motivated Stillman's heavy-handed ultimatum. But threatening to destroy Onyxx was unacceptable.

A man's work—his work—was his life. For sixteen years it was the only thing that had kept him going since Johanna's death. No one walked into his office, made threats to take that away, then stole one of his seasoned operatives out from under him without a fight.

Merrick picked up the phone and called the one person he knew who would be able to help him dig up the bone pile on Stillman. Peter Briggs had been a member of Merrick's unit when he'd first come to

Onyxx over twenty years ago. Peter had lost his legs on a mission that had gone sour, a mission that had damn near slaughtered their entire unit. Since then his old comrade spent his days in the Green Room keeping watch over the confidential files Onyxx kept under lock and key.

Adolf was sure Peter would be able to find out if Burgess Stillman had any skeletons in his closet.

"Peter, this is Merrick."

"What do you need?"

"Information on Burgess Stillman. He's SDECE."

"Anything in particular you're looking for?"

"Something he's shoved under the rug to keep himself looking clean. Hopefully a little dirt. I'd like this kept between us."

"You all right? You don't sound like yourself today."

"I've been better. Find me something and it'll improve my mood."

"I'll get right on it."

When he hung up the phone, Merrick stood and walked to the maps that covered one entire wall in his office. If he was Filip Petrov where would he go? Maybe a better question was, what unfinished business had Yurii left his brother to attend to?

A knock at the door interrupted Merrick's thoughts.

"Come in."

To his surprise it was Sly McEwen who stepped inside. Sly had taken an open-ended sabbatical close to a year ago. It was well deserved, but he was glad to see he was back.

"McEwen, I wondered when you were going to start missing us."

Sly grinned. "Old habits and all. You know how it goes."

"This place grows on a man. Ready to go back to work?"

"I'm ready."

"And Eva…did she come with you?"

"No. But she plans to join me in a few weeks."

"Then things are still good between you two?"

"She's an amazing woman."

Sly looked good, well-rested, and best of all, happy. Merrick was glad to see it. Sly deserved some happiness, and Eva deserved a man she could depend on. That would be Sly. He was one of the best he'd ever recruited.

His thoughts returning to the business at hand, he said, "I'm glad you're back. Perfect timing, in fact."

"I called Jacy and Bjorn. They updated me on what's been going on. The team has been busy. I heard Ash is back, too. I read about the hit on Petrov. I assume that was us."

"A collaboration with Quest. Sit down." Merrick climbed back behind his desk. "Pierce and Ash did a damn good job on that one. Of course we couldn't have done it without Quest's help. I won't take anything away from Polax and his beauty queens. Casmir Balasi was flawless in Italy."

Sly sat. "The femme fatale with the attitude. Bjorn mentioned her."

"Pierce is off on an overdue vacation at the moment, and I wouldn't be surprised if he's not spending it with Balasi."

"Pierce chasing after a woman? It's usually the other way around."

"Careful. Not too long ago you were chasing a woman. As I recall that was new territory for you, too."

Sly chuckled. "True enough. When a man finds a woman he can't live without, he's screwed."

"If he's lucky."

They shared the same grin.

Merrick leaned back in his chair. "Tell me something. How did you know that the corpse we impounded in Greece wasn't the Chameleon?"

"I didn't know for sure. It was just a hunch."

"Well, your hunch was right. We confirmed that the body is Paavo Creon. You might want to call Eva and let her know that. I know she's anxious to hear the particulars about her father. You have access to whatever you need. You can see Briggs about that."

"Then Paavo never died in that house fire twenty years ago?"

"No. It looks like he was held prisoner all that time by the Chameleon." Merrick grimaced. "I can't imagine what he endured all those years. How he was able to survive is beyond me."

"I think it suited the Chameleon to keep him alive. My take on the man is that he lives to torture his enemies. He can't do that if they're dead."

"You might be right about that. He's sure been torturing the hell out of me over the years."

"Now that we know he's alive, are you going after him again?"

"Definitely. He could still be in Greece, but it's hard to know where to start looking without a lead. He's a man who rarely makes a mistake. At the moment, however, I've got a new problem on my hands. One that involves Ash Kelly."

"What's going on with Ash? When I left he was still struggling over Sully's death, but I figured if he was back at work he'd made peace with that."

"He's put Sully's death behind him for the most part. I reactivated him a few weeks ago to help out Pierce on the Petrov mission, and he gave us a hundred percent."

"Then what's the problem?"

"You want the short version, or do you have time for a cup of coffee and some brainstorming?"

"Coffee is my passion. Second to Eva, that is."

As Merrick retrieved two cups, he asked, "How do you feel about going back into the field for a few weeks?"

"Why were you in prison, Mr. Toriago?"

Ash was standing at the window overlooking the city. He'd gotten Filip Petrov into bed with the help of the slender brunette with the green eyes. Filip had regained consciousness briefly, and was now sleeping as comfortably as could be expected considering a bullet wound.

He turned from the window. "I got caught being a naughty boy."

She was standing behind the couch in his plush suite. Dressed in loose black sweatpants and a gray T-shirt, she looked a little lost among the heavy brocade drapes and gold walls. The curved white couch was damn near the size of the limo he'd rented.

She had washed the blood off her face and what

remained was a half-inch cut on her left cheek and three small scratches on her chin. She'd been lucky. He wondered if she was aware of just how lucky.

Now that he was able to get a better look at her, he could see that she was rip-cord lean. Almost too thin.

"How naughty?"

"How naughty do you want me to be, *señorita?*"

"Do you always look at a woman that way?"

"What way?"

"Like you're envisioning her naked."

"Only the pretty ones."

She arched her eyebrows over her dramatic eyes. And they were spectacular. The oddest shade of green he'd ever seen.

"I checked to see if there's another room in the hotel. There will be an opening tomorrow."

She rounded the couch. The room's amber lighting captured her trim figure as she slipped behind the bar. She went on a search, disappearing from sight for a moment. When she popped back up, she asked, "Don't you have anything to drink?"

"What do you want?"

"Something besides water and," she bent over again, then back up, "tea. You drink tea?"

"I do. I'll have something sent up. Anything in particular?"

"A nice dry wine and some gin."

"A party girl."

She gazed at him from across the bar, her expression giving away nothing. "Don't get excited. I like things quiet and uncomplicated. When I drink, I usually drink alone."

"Not with Petrov?"

"With Filip, too."

"A one-man woman who likes to curl up on the couch." He sighed. "I should be so lucky."

She didn't answer back, simply stared him down, looking him over with the eyes of someone who was sizing up the enemy.

"I would rethink moving out. Someone wants Filip dead."

"That's not your problem."

"That's right, you know how to handle a gun."

"Filip recognized your name, but I'm afraid I don't. Should I?"

"I don't know why you should. I'm just a business-man."

"A naughty business man with merchandise to sell. The kind of merchandise that puts a man in prison."

Ash grinned. "I was young and reckless in the old days. What can I say? I trusted the wrong people."

"A mistake I don't plan to make."

She rounded the bar and sat down on the couch. It made her look like a little girl among the oversized cushions, and he wondered if she was one of those women who starved herself.

"Salavich is a syndicate man. Filip mentioned your father was the head of a cartel." Her eyes drifted over him again. More sizing up. "What is it? Drugs, or are you in the white slave market? Or perhaps it's some-thing much bigger?"

Ash had thought he was through digging up the skeletons of his old life, but it had become part of his cover. From production to distribution, Estabon's business sense had been pure genius and he'd taught his son everything he knew.

Illegal, yes, but it had paid off with staggering wealth. In those days he hadn't thought about the right or wrong of it. Money to burn. Excess in all things.

It had been a risky business, and it had gained them more enemies than Hitler. But it wasn't an enemy who had betrayed the Toriago family eight years ago. He was being honest when he told her that he'd trusted the wrong people. In the same way a traitor had betrayed Stillman, there had been a double-cross in play on a drug delivery that had cost the Toriago family everything. And the man responsible had been as close to him as a brother.

"Some women like mystery men. I'm not one of them, Mr. Toriago."

"And some men like pushy women. If I'm getting the action, and the ride of my life, there isn't anything better than a pushy woman with good hip action. If you decide you want to play that game, maybe I'll feel like sharing my life story. But sharing goes two ways."

"As you said, I'm a one-man woman."

She didn't mince words. But being beautiful and direct wasn't going to keep her alive. She had no idea what kind of danger she was in. She had picked the wrong boyfriend if she wanted to live to a ripe old age.

"If I were you, I'd be more curious about who and why the car you were riding in today was ambushed instead of who and what I am."

"There could be another explanation for that. Maybe the shooter was after you. Maybe he made a mistake and hit the wrong car. You arrived at Ballvaro only minutes after we did."

"I have no enemies here."

"But you don't deny you have enemies?"

"Who doesn't? As far as the shooter goes, we're just going to have to be patient."

"You think he'll strike again."

"*Sì*. And it will be soon. That's why you need to stay here."

"Because you can protect us."

"Filip is vulnerable at the moment."

"I can protect him."

"You and your little gun?"

She shoved her hair away from her face and leaned her head back against the couch and closed her eyes. "All right, Toriago. For now, we'll stay here." She opened her eyes. "Happy?"

"I would be happier if you weren't a one-woman man." Ash grinned. "You know my name, *señorita*, but I don't know yours."

"Allegra."

"Well, Allegra, you relax and take a nap, and I'll be back shortly."

"Back? Where are you going?"

"Petrov will need sterile bandages and some pain killers. He's going to have an uncomfortable night. There's a shop in the lobby."

She sat up. "I'll go."

"Don't you want to stay close to Filip? Maybe I'm a liar and while you're gone I'll slit his throat."

"As you said, you've gone to a lot of trouble to keep Filip alive. I don't think you have murder on your mind." She stood. "Everything we owned was destroyed today in the car explosion. I could use a change of clothes, and a few other things."

"You can use my toothbrush."

"I'd prefer my own."

"Suit yourself."

She hesitated.

"Is there something else?"

"Money. If you could lend me some, I'll see that you get it back."

"That would require trust."

"I'll owe you, and I always pay my debts."

"You already owe me."

"Then I'll owe you double?"

"I like the sound of that. Charge whatever you need to my room number, *señorita*."

In her French accent she said, "*Gracias,* Señor Toriago," then started for the door.

"Allegra?"

She turned. "Yes?"

"You're not going to run off, are you?"

"One-man woman, remember? What I want is right here."

Allegra exited the elevator, spied the small shop in the lobby, and entered it. She picked up sterile bandages and pain pills for Filip, then a few necessities—deodorant, two toothbrushes, a hairbrush and comb. A lipstick and compact.

She left the shop and located a men's clothing store and bought Filip a gray sweater, a pair of jeans, underwear and socks. She noticed a trendy boutique with leather boots and fur coats in one window, and sexy, colorful lingerie in the other. There she bought a pair of jeans for herself and a black turtleneck, an off-the-shoulder white sweater, tall black boots, and a few pairs of underwear.

On the way to the checkout, a cashmere hat and leather belt caught her eye. Tossing them on her pile, she glanced out the window and noticed a man loitering outside the door wearing a long trench coat and hat, the brim pulled low enough to conceal his face.

She touched the cut on her cheek, her thoughts returning to the ambush at Ballvaro. If this was the shooter then Toriago had been right—they were going to be hit again.

She finished making her purchases, wishing she'd taken her gun with her, but she'd left it in the drawer on the nightstand beside Filip's bed. On her way back to the elevator she pretended to window shop. The mystery man did the same.

If she got onto the elevator and he joined her, what then?

She went past the elevators, realizing now that she was going to need some help to shake him. She entered the hotel bar and lounge, a modern den of red booths, gold tables, and a shiny circular bar. It was as extravagant as the hotel's suites, and the crowd was dressed just as extreme. She stuck out like a homeless vagrant in a ballroom.

This would be no help at all.

She quickly disappeared in the crowd looking for the rest room sign.

She entered a short hall, then disappeared into the

bathroom. There she pulled the sexy white sweater from the bag, as well as the jeans. She changed into the new clothes, stuffed the old ones into the bag, then pulled on the high boots, and wrapped the wide black belt around her slender waist. Digging deeper into the bag, she found the cashmere hat, gave her shoulder-length hair a twist, then tucked it under the black hat, pulling it off-side.

A little swipe with the compact, a touch of lip gloss, and two minutes later she left the bathroom looking like a style-conscious party girl in need of a drink to unwind from a long day.

It was true, it had been a long day and she was in need of a drink. She hadn't been allowed one drop during her training.

She lingered in the hall, and when a party of three women left the bathroom she moved with them, then slid onto a stool at the bar.

She spotted the trench coat seated at a table near the entrance. After what had happened today, she knew it was the shooter, her training, past and present, giving her an edge.

Why he was after Filip remained a mystery. But after what had happened at Nescosto, she knew he must be the target.

Unsure her disguise would hold, she ordered a gin martini from the bartender then asked him if she could use the bar phone. When he hesitated she gave him a sexy smile, then winked. He handed her the phone, winking back. She asked him how she could reach suite 811, and he was only too happy to help her after she touched his hand and complimented him on his watch.

She didn't want to call Toriago, but this was no time to gamble on a weak disguise.

"*Hola.*"

"I need you to come down here."

"Allegra?"

"Yes, it's me. I'm in the bar, and—"

"I thought you were on a mission to buy medical supplies for Filip."

"I was, but now I'm in the bar trying to shake my tail."

"*Sì*, a party girl. I was right."

"Tail as in being followed. I think it's this afternoon's shooter."

"I'll be right there."

"Wait, I have something else to tell you. Toriago? Toriago—"

It took Ash a long ten minutes to recognize her. She had changed clothes. Why in the hell hadn't she mentioned that on the phone?

He'd called Naldo and had him come up to the suite to babysit Filip while he went out.

As he moved through the crowd toward the bar, he scanned the faces, but it was hard to flag anyone without knowing who he was looking for.

He closed in on Allegra. He liked a woman in jeans and boots. A woman who was full of surprises. She was certainly a surprise. The white sweater exposed bare shoulders, and the soft black hat made her profile sharp and her green eyes even sexier than before.

"Another, miss?" The bartender asked.

"Yes. I'm waiting for someone and he's late."

"He's here now." Ash slid his hand along her trim waist. "*Hola*. You look…different."

She turned slowly on the barstool. "You hung up too soon. I was going to tell you I'd changed."

"Let's find a booth."

"I thought you came to get me out of here."

"And I will, but we don't want to lead our friend to our door, do we?" He tugged her off the barstool, but when she bent down to retrieve the bag, he said, "Leave it."

"But—"

"The new look might fool your admirer, but the bag won't."

Ash gave the bag a kick and sent it farther beneath the bar. Then he took her arm and led her across the room to a dark booth that allowed him to see every corner of the crowded bar.

When she slid into the booth along the wall, Ash followed her. Sucking close as if they were a couple, he asked, "Where is he?"

"Over there. The table by the door. The trench coat wearing the hat."

"Do you recognize him?"

"No. But that doesn't mean anything. I don't know Filip's enemies."

The admission could mean she hadn't been with Filip that long, or that he didn't share his business with her. The one thing Ash knew for sure was that she was handling the situation like a pro. She was calm and composed just like when she was in the car and he'd put the pressure on.

That only came with practice.

"Our friend must be recognizable to someone or he wouldn't be working so hard to disguise himself."

"I thought that, too."

The waitress came by. Allegra ordered another martini and Ash ordered a Coke.

"You don't drink? That was why the bar in your suite was empty."

"No, I don't drink."

She tasted her drink. Savored her. "Moderation is the key to life's little evils. A man who indulges in excess is a weak man."

"I admit to few weaknesses, but liquor and beautiful women can be a deadly combination, so I've given up liquor."

That brought a smile to her face, and he smiled back, then glanced toward the door. The trench coat hadn't moved.

Time lagged.

Ash touched her bare shoulder. "Is this your normal style?"

"I can be whatever I need to be."

"Right now you need to be my woman. Move a little closer."

"We should be getting back to Filip. He could wake up and try to get out of bed."

"He won't be getting out of bed tonight."

"You don't know him."

"How well do you?"

"Well enough to know that he won't stay down long. Look. He's leaving."

They watched the trench coat stand and step away from the table, but he never left. Instead he began to stroll through the bar searching the faces in the crowd.

"He's coming this way." Ash tucked her deeper into the booth to hide her.

"Now what?"

Ash turned to study the body beneath the trench coat. If it was a man, he was shorter than most, with more of a sauntering gait than a swagger.

The picture Stillman had given him of Jazmin Grant popped in his head. The blonde was five-seven and curvy in all the right places. Just maybe their friend was a woman. If Grant was here, that would shorten his mission.

"He's getting closer," Allegra said. "We need to get out of here."

"If we get up, he'll tag you for sure." Ash slid his arm around her and pulled her against him.

"What are you doing?"

"Saving you...again." He lowered his head and brushed her lips with his, paused, then kissed her again.

"It's time to say thank you. And be convincing. Perhaps even a little excessive. You're a one-man woman, remember, and right now, I'm that man."

Chapter 5

Ash shoved Allegra into his suite and followed after her, but not before he looked back to make sure that they weren't being followed. They had slipped out of the hotel lounge after the trench coat had given up and left the bar.

He had been torn whether to take chase, or get Allegra back upstairs. If it was Grant, and she was working alone, he should have confronted her then and there, but he couldn't be sure it was her, or that she was acting alone. Then there was his cover to consider.

He'd made the only decision he could make at the time, to protect Allegra first and hope that he'd be able to locate Grant afterward.

He closed the door just as Naldo rolled off the couch. "Everything okay, *prim*—boss?"

"Who's he?"

"How's Petrov?"

"Still sleeping."

She spun around. "I said, who is he?"

"Allegra, meet Naldo."

She glanced back at his cousin, gave him a long hard look. "You're the…chauffeur. The guy who drives like he's on speed."

"*Sì*. Chauffeur. Errand boy. Watch dog. Vigorous bull… It's a pleasure, *señorita*."

Naldo was grinning like a puppet on a string. The truth was, he loved women—all women. In the old days he hadn't gone a day without a different face in his bed. Well, Toriago hadn't either, not until he'd met Lolita.

The old memories surfaced, and they were as unexpected as the hard-on that had been dropped in his lap downstairs when Allegra had kissed him in the bar.

He had felt dead for close to a year, but with one kiss, Filip's woman had plugged him in and turned him on. It was like lightning had struck and his body had suddenly gone off strike, or at least had awakened from a long sleep.

As much as he would have liked to celebrate the fact that he was back in business, he was the first to admit that this wasn't the time to be thinking about sex and personal achievements.

"You all right, boss?"

Ash blinked out of his muse. "Wait for me in the hall, Naldo. I'll be right there." After his cousin left, he said, "Stay in the suite with Petrov. Don't leave for any reason."

"Are you going back to the bar for my bag?"

"The bag isn't important right now."

"But—"

"Lock the door and don't let anyone in."

"Does that include you?"

She had her chin hiked in the air and her hands planted on her slender hips. She really did look good in those jeans.

Ash grabbed his leather jacket off the back of the couch. "I've got a key. I'll let myself in."

He left the suite, then headed for the elevator with Naldo.

"Where are we going, *primo?*"

"On a witch hunt. Today's shooter could be in the hotel."

In the elevator Ash gave Naldo a quick rundown on what had happened in the bar. When they reached the lobby, he pulled his phone from his pocket and hit a button. In seconds the picture of Jazmin Grant popped up on his screen.

"Here's what she looks like. If she ditched the disguise you'll be looking for a brown-eyed blonde with killer curves. If I'm wrong, keep your eyes open for a trench coat wearing a hat."

Together they searched the hotel, but after two hours, Ash had no choice but to give up.

"Sonofabitch."

"You want me to keep looking, *primo?*"

"Hang out in the bar a while. Maybe she'll show back up. I'm going to get some air and check around outside."

While Naldo headed for the bar, Ash exited the hotel. It was dark out and colder. He pulled up the collar on his jacket, lit a cigarette, and crossed the street. He should have been dissecting the situation with Jazmin Grant, but instead he found himself thinking about Allegra and the moment she had put her arms around his neck and kissed him with enough lip suction to clean a clogged pipe—his pipe.

It was as he started into the second block that he picked up a tail. Ash tossed his cigarette and ducked into an alley. Like clockwork, his shadow followed him.

In the alley he found an alcove and slipped into it. He didn't pull his gun—there was no need. The minute the shadow entered the alley, Ash stepped out to confront him.

"You're slipping, old man."

When Sly McEwen drew closer, Ash saw he was wearing a grin.

"If my intention was to keep you in the dark, you still would be."

That was probably true. Ash had a wealth of respect for his Onyxx comrade. Sly was as smart as he was tough.

"I saw you in the bar."

"I saw you, too."

"What are you doing here?" Ash asked.

"Merrick's idea."

"To keep an eye on me?"

"He's had you followed since you left Washington. I took over this morning."

Ash leaned against the building. "I know Merrick is territorial when it comes to his men, but I told him that I could—"

"He knows you can handle yourself. It's Stillman he's worried about. He doesn't trust him."

"That makes two of us."

"Three. After hearing what he pulled I don't like him, and I don't even know him. I think Merrick's feeling guilty over what you're sacrificing for Onyxx."

"He doesn't need to. You would have done the same thing."

"Maybe. Anyway, I'm here to watch your ass, and to make sure Petrov stays alive. The data you and Pierce took from Nescosto proves that the Petrov brothers were laundering the Chameleon's money. At the moment it's the only lead we have to getting that bastard. You know Merrick, everything he does circles back to the Chameleon."

"Did you see what happened this afternoon at Ballvaro?"

"I was there. Tell me Petrov's alive."

"He took a hit, but he'll live. He's in my suite."

"Talk about timing."

"Yeah, I couldn't have planned it better. Merrick's not the only one interested in Petrov. Stillman needs him alive, too."

"What's Stillman's interest?"

"I'm on a recovery mission. Stolen data from the SDECE."

"Who's the brunette with the sweet mouth, and what does she have to do with it?"

"Her name's Allegra, but I don't know how she figures in yet."

"At least the working conditions aren't too painful."

Ash smiled. "I'll admit that she's easy on the eyes."

He explained the subterfuge that had gone on in the bar. He might have tried to explain it too much by the look on Sly's face—his grin never wavered. He finished with, "She claims she's Filip's woman."

"You don't buy it?"

"Petrov's gay. At least that's what it says in his profile."

"Maybe he likes variety in his bed."

"I don't think so."

"What makes you say that?"

"Just a feeling."

It was more than a feeling, but Ash wasn't going to go into that with Sly until he tested out his theory first. He'd learned something in the bar, and it would require a little experiment later.

Sly asked, "What about this stolen data?"

"A rogue agent at the SDECE sold them out. The disk is full of access codes. Stillman thinks Filip is here to have Casso Salavich decode the information. I'm suppose to infiltrate Salavich's organization, locate the data before it can be deciphered, then run down Jazmin Grant and bring both back to Stillman."

"Grant? Didn't she die at Nescosto?"

"Stillman thinks she's alive, and I'm starting to believe that he's right. I think she's here."

"Here?"

"I think Grant could be this afternoon's shooter, and the tail Allegra picked up that followed her into the bar in the lobby. I wanted to flag you, but I couldn't chance blowing my cover. Why she's here, I don't know. Maybe she's trying to get the disk back, or maybe she was double-crossed. I won't know that until I find her."

"If Petrov has the data on him—"

"He doesn't. I checked."

"Could it have been destroyed when his car blew up this afternoon?"

"It's possible, but for now, I've got to believe it's still out there."

"How does Stillman plan for you to get inside Salavich's organization? When I was at Ballvaro this afternoon, I counted over two dozen guards. The grounds are pruned lean—that means there are surveillance cameras. Damn hard to get in without being seen or setting off an alarm."

"Somehow Stillman learned who I am."

"What do you mean, who you are?"

"Before Onyxx, I was someone else."

"Weren't we all."

"I changed my name when I came to Onyxx. It wouldn't have worked any other way. I'm the son of Estabon Toriago. My father controlled eighty percent of the drug traffic in Mexico before his death. When you talk to Merrick tell him that Marco Toriago has risen from the ashes and is about to get back in the drug trade with Casso Salavich. At least that's my cover."

Sly joined Ash against the wall in the alley and lit a cigarette. "Is that why you were there this afternoon?"

"I called him when I arrived yesterday. He invited me to Ballvaro for a meeting."

"Then all hell broke loose with the shooter."

"That's right."

Sly dug in his pocket and pulled out an electronic tracker. "Can you plant this bug on Petrov? That way we can keep him close."

"I don't need it. I've already tagged him. But he won't be leaving the hotel too soon. He can't even get out of bed right now. Still, if and when he does, we'll be able to follow his every move."

"What room are you in?"

"811. And you?"

"412."

"Stay out of sight, and I'll contact you when I know something."

"Who's your friend?"

"You mean Naldo? He's my cousin. I needed some backup. He's posing as my chauffeur. He's cool under fire." Ash grinned. "But I guess I should have known that Merrick wouldn't leave me out in the cold. I'm glad you're here. Do me a favor and run a check on Jazmin Grant. Stillman gave me her profile, but it's full of holes. He's covering something up and I want to know what it is."

Allegra checked on Filip again. Toriago had been gone over two hours and she moved quietly into the room. He was still sleeping, and she walked to the bed and sat down beside him. She slowly pulled back the sheet. He stirred, moaned, but didn't wake up.

The wound looked horrible, charred flesh and blackened blood. It needed to be cleaned, then bandaged. She could have done it if she hadn't left her bag at the bar.

She left the bedroom. She was getting tired of not knowing the reason she was in Budapest. She didn't trust Filip. Not like she had Yurii. She should call Cyrus and tell him that Filip had been shot. Surely he would either give her a reason to stay, or tell her to fly back to Athens.

She knew who Casso Salavich was. Knew he was a powerful man in the criminal world in Europe. Perhaps they were there to take him down?

She didn't like being kept in the dark, and she didn't like the situation of owing a stranger for his hospitality—a stranger who was into nasty business.

The direction of her thoughts took a sudden turn, and Allegra touched her lips. Toriago wasn't all talk and smooth moves. He knew how to kiss a woman and make her remember it. Make her want more. She couldn't blame him entirely for what had happened. She had kissed him back downstairs, and she had played the game perfectly.

But that game wouldn't have been necessary if she knew why the hell she was in Budapest. The bottom line was she was going to call Cyrus and demand a few answers. And the sooner the better, while Filip was still on his back.

She took a shower. Toriago hadn't said where he was going, but she suspected he'd gone looking for the mystery man in the trench coat. Out of the shower, she dried her hair, then found Toriago's shaving kit and rummaged through it. He'd been telling the truth about an antibiotic for her cut. She used it, along with his toothbrush—after all, he had offered it to her.

She left the bathroom wearing the white robe she'd found behind the door—compliments of the hotel.

Toriago still wasn't back when she strolled into the living room. She found wine and gin behind the small half-circle bar. He must have had some sent up while she was in the lobby. She poured a glass of wine and stepped out on the balcony.

The moon was out and the cool air made her shiver. She tugged the ends of the white robe together, pulled up the collar. Sipped the wine.

The city lights sent a golden glow over the street below. Budapest was beautiful at night, a place she would enjoy if she were on her own time. She could see the shadow of the Buda Hills in the distance, Parliament, and the Danube at its narrowest as it passed through the city.

It was by luck that she was on the balcony when Toriago exited the alley. She watched him cross the street and head back to the hotel. His lazy sauntering gait was back.

Yes, she'd noticed his confident stride, just like she'd noticed everything else, from his nice ass and power-house shoulders to his hard abdomen. Scars and all, he had the complete package.

But he was about more than a great body, a handsome face, and excellent taste in hotel suites. He had spent time in prison, and was about to climb into bed with Casso Salavich.

She was caught up in watching Toriago when another man exited the same alley. She studied the second man. He didn't cross the street. Instead he flagged a taxi.

She was still standing on the balcony, wrapped in a white robe fifteen minutes later when Toriago came through the front door carrying the bag he'd insisted she leave behind in the bar. She came back into the living room sliding the balcony door shut.

"Do you have a death wish?"

"Meaning?"

"I'd just as soon not everyone know we're on the eighth floor. Someone blew up your car, and a few hours ago you were followed. Standing out there wearing that is like waving a flag. You could be picked off from across the street."

"Afraid for me, or yourself?"

"I'd like to avoid being shot today if I can."

"You're a tough guy. Prison memories and a big bad scar. What's one more to add to your bragging rights?"

He set her bag down next to the couch. "Have any scars you'd like to show me and brag about?"

She had a couple, but they weren't worth bragging about. Actually she couldn't remember where she'd gotten them.

"Why was Filip at Salavich's bastion today?"

That was a very good question, she thought. Allegra cautioned herself not to say too much. She was supposed to be Filip's woman, nothing more, and until she contacted Cyrus she would continue the ruse.

"He doesn't discuss his business with me."

"And you're all right with that?"

"Why wouldn't I be?"

"I don't think you're the kind of woman who goes into anything blind. You handled yourself pretty good downstairs."

"Just pretty good?"

"The disguise was quick thinking."

"Since we're on that subject, I think it would be best if Filip was spared the details."

"You want me to lie to him?"

"I don't see any reason to upset him with details that aren't important."

He eyed the robe, then the belt tied around her waist. "Sharing secrets with you would be my pleasure, *señorita.*"

The look he was giving her told her that his silence was going to cost her. She didn't like his wolf's grin any more than she liked her position right now. If Filip thought he couldn't trust her, then what?

She'd been going over in her mind the time she'd spent with him the past few days and the one thing that stuck out was Filip standing on his yacht with a detonator in his hand, the *Sera Vedette* on fire and the captain fish bait.

She finished her wine and set the glass on the bar. Turning slowly, she asked, "What would it take for you to forget what happened downstairs?"

"I rarely forget anything. I have a healthy memory."

"Your price, Toriago?"

"As I recall, your cash flow is tight at the moment."

"Then why don't you tell me what you have in mind."

"There is one thing." He grinned.

It was a self-serving naughty grin, akin to a dog's after he'd cornered a fox.

"You're saying if I sleep with you, it will cancel my debts, and make you forget what happened in the bar?"

"Is that what you're offering?"

Allegra walked to the couch and sat. Curling her legs beneath her, she studied Toriago, wondering who he had met in the alley. Wondered if she slept with him if she would be digging herself a deeper hole, or if his healthy memory would suddenly turn fuzzy.

"I think the ball is in your court, *señorita.*"

"I'm thinking."

"About whether you can trust me or not?"

"I don't do trust. I do cause and effect. We make a deal, and if you break it, then—"

"Then you kill me with your gun when my back is turned."

Allegra smiled. "You've played this game before. Good."

He took off his jacket, tossed it on a chair. Her eyes locked on it, pictured the phone in his pocket. She decided before the night was over that she would call Cyrus.

Before he sat down across from her, he pulled his shirt from his pants and unbuttoned it. He lit a cigarette, leaned forward and tossed the lighter on the coffee table between them, and reached for the ashtray. "Could you do it?"

"Do what?"

"Kill me? I'm still going over in my mind the whole trust, cause and effect thing."

She tried to keep her eyes from drifting to his open shirt. "Some business is more unpleasant than others. But survival is survival."

"Whether it requires that you shoot a man or sleep with him?"

"Filip wouldn't like what happened downstairs. I see no reason to upset him after the bad day he's already had. I'll tell Filip about the tail I picked up. I think he should know that the shooter could be here. But the rest—"

"Do you think you're up to it?"

"Excuse me?"

"Downstairs it seemed like that kiss took a lot out of you."

"Are you saying it was lacking?"

"Let's just say under less pressure and some rest I would hope you could do better. Of course there could be another explanation."

"And that is?"

"Has it been a while since you slept with Filip?"

"Why do you ask?"

"Like I said. You seemed a bit out of practice. One minute you were hot, then you were cold. Well, I don't know Filip, but some men aren't very good when it comes to knowing what a woman wants or needs. You can't be blamed for that."

Allegra sank into the couch a little deeper. Yes, it had been a while, but in her business there wasn't much time for personal gratification—routine bred acceptance—yet that had nothing to do with her performance tonight. She had been at the top of her game, and if he didn't think so then maybe he was the one who was out of practice.

"Maybe I just don't like you, Toriago."

"But you're still willing to sleep with me?" He shook his head. "No, I don't think that's it. There must be something about me that you like or you wouldn't be willing to sacrifice so much."

"An oversized ego usually means a man's been shortchanged in another area." She smiled. "You have my sympathy."

He grinned, the wolf was back. "There's only one way to find out."

"Perhaps I'll tell Filip the truth and save you the

embarrassment. Who did you meet after you left the hotel? I saw you step out of the alley. I was on the balcony, remember?"

"I didn't meet anyone."

"I saw a man leave the alley less than a minute after you, and it wasn't your chauffeur."

"I went looking for our friend in the trench coat, and when I didn't find…*him,* I searched the surrounding area. After that, I went to the bar and got your bag. Trust me, I didn't meet anyone."

"As I said, trust isn't something I do. My mother raised me to be a realist. She said never trust a man you haven't known forever. Since forever is an untouchable, unreachable phenomenon for a man, you can understand my dilemma."

She uncurled her legs and got off the couch. She started past him, but he reached out and grabbed her arm and stopped her.

"I can get you out of here. Find you a safe place if that's what you need. If you're afraid of Petrov—"

She pulled away. "I'm not."

He stood, reached up and brushed his thumb over the cut on her cheek. "I notice everything. You don't know him as well as you pretend to. It's in your eyes when you look at him."

"You're mistaken if you think that's what you see."

His thumb stroked her temple. "It's not everyday a woman agrees to sleep with a stranger to keep a minor secret from her boyfriend. Whatever you need to walk away from, I can help." He dropped his hand. "The offer has no time limit."

"You're a contradiction, Toriago. One minute your

eyes are stripping me naked, and the next minute you're playing Boy Scout. You see, I can read eyes, too. I can also read body language." Allegra shifted her attention to Toriago's crotch. "As lacking as my performance was downstairs, I managed to do something right. And for the record, when I'm wrong, I say so. I can see that you haven't been shortchanged. My mistake."

Allegra picked up the bag next to the couch and escaped into the bedroom. When she closed the door behind her and turned, she found Filip awake.

"I'm thirsty. Get me some water."

"Of course. I brought you some pain killers." She left the room and retrieved a glass of water from the bathroom, then stepped back into the bedroom. She sat down beside him and gave him the pills and held the water glass for him.

"The wound should be cleaned and bandaged." She touched his forehead. "You have a fever."

"Where are we?"

"You don't remember?"

"If I did I wouldn't be asking."

"We're in Toriago's suite. I didn't know where to take you. He suggested we stay with him."

"Why would he be so generous?"

"I don't know. But when I went downstairs to get you some clean clothes and the medical supplies, I was followed. It could be the shooter from this afternoon. I think it's good that we're here. That way—"

"You don't think until you're told to think." His eyes drifted over her. "Why are you wearing his robe?"

"I took a shower. But the robe isn't—"

"To wash his scent off you?"

"What?"

"I saw the way you looked at him in the car. The way you looked at his body, and the way he was looking at you. He would have taken you in the car in front of me if I had told him he could have you."

She opened her mouth to deny it, but in a split second Filip grabbed her around the neck, his fingers digging deeply into her flesh. He squeezed harder— hard enough to cut off her air supply.

Allegra reached up to pry his hand away, but he pulled her down beside him, his fingers still squeezing the life out of her. He sat up and leaned over her, his strength coming out of nowhere, considering the shape he was in.

"I thought I told you how we were going to play this game. You are my woman. We're here on business, nothing else, so stay away from Toriago. Now go put some clothes on."

When Filip released her she rolled off the bed choking and gasping for air, clutching her bruised throat. She felt dizzy as she struggled up from her knees and she backed up and used the wall to steady herself. She tried to speak, but she couldn't breathe.

"Did you hear me? Get some clothes on, then bandage up this damn wound."

Chapter 6

Allegra heard the shower turn on, and quickly rose from the couch. She hurried down the hall, past the bathroom and slipped into Toriago's bedroom.

After Filip had nearly choked her to death she had decided calling Cyrus was the only thing she could do. She should have called him sooner.

In the bedroom she hurried to the bed, switched on the light that sat on the nightstand, then quickly scanned the room. Toriago's leather jacket was draped over a chair.

Right pocket.

Got it.

She pulled out the phone and quickly punched in the code number. It started to ring.

Once.

Twice.

She heard the shower turn off.

A third ring.

Number four.

Dammit, answer the phone.

On the sixth ring the voice mail turned on.

She had no choice but to leave a message, then disconnect. She slid the phone back into the pocket of Toriago's jacket, then turned to leave. But it was too late. The bathroom door opened.

There was only one way out of the bedroom. Caught in the act, she scrambled to the bed and sat down just as Toriago walked into the room wearing a pair of black PJ bottoms and nothing else.

The look on his face when he saw her seated on the bed was priceless. It was complete surprise, and then it turned wary as he glanced around the room. "What are you doing in here?"

The truth would damn her. A lame excuse would be worse. She thought about making a joke and trying to be funny. It wasn't really her style, and anyway she didn't see anything funny about the day's events, or the fact that Filip had nearly killed her a few hours ago.

In the end, she said, "I owe you for saving my life… twice, remember?"

He angled his head, took in her appearance. She didn't look like she was there to seduce him—she had changed back into her jeans and the black sweater she'd bought downstairs. But she'd turned him on wearing jeans before.

"Then you really are a woman who pays her debts no matter what the price."

She had declined eating with him when he'd ordered up a late supper. She didn't think she could swallow, and it still hurt to talk.

Keeping her voice in check, seeing a way out, she said, "Most men would find that an admirable quality. Since you're not one of them, I'll say goodnight."

She stood, started past him and almost made it out the door when he stopped her. Pulling her around to face him, keeping his eyes locked on hers, he closed the door.

There was a moment of awkward silence, then he curled his hand around the back of her neck and pulled her into his space. The pressure on her neck was excruciating, but she refused to make a sound.

He dipped his head and kissed her, pulled back, and said, "I guess I'm a lucky man tonight."

"Then we have a deal?"

He searched her face, looked into her eyes.

"Is it there? Can you read my eyes? If you can, then you know I'm not playing a game."

He didn't answer. Instead he released her and walked over to the desk. He picked up his jacket and pulled out his phone. In that moment she thought it was all over. That he knew why she was in his room. But he only checked his messages, then turned off the phone and set it on the desk.

Facing her, he said with a smile, "It would be a shame to be interrupted. Take off your sweater."

He didn't waste time, and she was all for getting it over with. She might enjoy looking at his body, but until now she hadn't considered what he would think of hers.

She was thinner than she had ever been. Not as curvy, and her breasts were a small handful.

Still, she'd given him a hard-on once before, and at the moment it was rising to the occasion again. In fact, it was giving a parade performance that could flag a train.

"Second thoughts?"

"No." She pulled off her sweater and dropped it to the floor.

His eyes went straight to her breasts covered in blue satin, and she felt her nipples constrict in response to his stare down.

"Now the jeans."

She kicked off her shoes, unzipped her pants and slid them past her thighs. She bent over, pushed them down her legs and stepped out of them leaving her in a blue thong.

He didn't bait her again. Instead he walked toward her and circled her as if he was deciding whether she was worth taking to bed or not. Again she wondered if he thought she was too thin. She couldn't explain how she'd lost the weight. She'd just woken up one morning and she was twenty pounds thinner.

She refocused her energy as he circled her again. Whatever his eccentricities were, she would meet them head on.

He stopped behind her and unhooked her bra. His hands on her shoulders, he slowly slid the straps off her shoulders.

The air was cool in the room, and she realized that she was giving him a parade performance, too.

"What happened to your neck?"

She touched the bruise on her throat. "It must have happened this afternoon during the ambush."

He ran his hand down her spine and she closed her eyes. He'd gotten her out of her clothes so fast she had thought the rest would be quick, too. She didn't expect foreplay. In fact, she was surprised by it.

If he thought she didn't understand by now the way a man's mind and body worked, he was wrong. Just because a woman needed more than the act to be satisfied, didn't change the facts, or the one-two-three code men lived by whether they realized it or not.

Men are all action, baby doll. Get hard, get in, get out. The next thing you know they're snoring or pulling on their pants and having a cigarette.

His warm hands continued to play with her, tease her flesh and arouse her insides in ways she wasn't prepared for. Right now she didn't need an exception to Bonnie's rules on men and sex. The act, she could handle. It would just be sex, and then her debt to him would be paid, and hopefully by tomorrow she and Filip would be gone. That is, if he was strong enough to get out of bed. He'd certainly had a surge of energy when he'd tried to choke her.

But as the minutes ticked slowly by Toriago continued to break the rules. Continued to touch her and stroke her body until she felt as if she was going to melt into a pool on the floor.

She turned around. "Stop. Really, you don't have to waste time getting me ready. I'm ready."

"You're ready for what?"

"To repay my debt."

"What's your rush? We have all night." His hands drifted over her bare shoulders, and then one finger traced a slow path over the width of one breast to the other, brushing her nipples.

"I'm a get in, get out, kind of girl," she finally said. "Really?"

"Yes, really." She ran her hand down his chest and boldly cupped him. "I think you're more than ready, so—"

"Maybe you should make sure. Put your hand in my pants."

He was watching her for a reaction. She hesitated only a second, then slowly slid her hand inside and touched him, curling her fingers around him.

This time it was her turn to check out his reaction. He sucked in a ragged breath, then his arm tightened around her. She could feel him pulsing in her hand as she stroked him, hear every breath he took.

"You're more than ready. In fact, you feel like you're in pain," she whispered.

"More than you know." He nuzzled her ear, and his smooth cheek brushed her face. Suddenly, he asked, "Do you always do whatever you're told?"

"Is this a trick question?"

"Your answer is supposed to be, 'Only when you're the one asking.'"

"Sorry. I didn't realize I was feeding your ego as well as your—"

He kissed her before she could finish what she was going to say. And while he played with her lips, she played with him.

Good old foreplay. The magic pill to bringing a woman to her knees. Only she wasn't going to let it happen. She wasn't going to feel anything for this man.

The minute she made herself that promise, the kiss turned erotic, and she realized she was in trouble.

He was turning this into something more than just sex. He was getting to know her body, and likewise she was learning his. He was getting into her head, and that was too intimate.

She pulled her hand away from him. "Enough of this."

"No." He slid his hand over her back and down her hips, his fingers cupping her small ass. Stroking her, he pulled her flush against him and rotated his hips.

The scent of him, his hands on her… It was too much and she arched against him, suddenly wanting him to take his time. Wanting this slow seduction to go on all night no matter what the price.

Her hands went around him and she stroked his broad back, felt his smooth flesh and the bulk of his muscles beneath her fingertips.

His heart was pounding in his chest, or was it hers?

When he broke the kiss, he stepped away from her and walked to the bed. Pulling back the sheet, he said, "After you."

She climbed onto the mattress wearing only her panties and lay down. His gaze found hers, then it drifted downward, over her slender neck, her naked breasts—farther to the junction of her thighs.

When he sat down beside her, she did all she could do not to reach for him. Her stomach was in a fever knot, and her insides were screaming for him to put his hands on her again.

She hadn't been with a man in a long time. That had to be the reason why she was aching so badly, so hot for him.

"You're not afraid of me?"

"No."

"And you're not afraid of Petrov?"

"I already told you I'm not."

"Not even when he tried to choke you." He laid his hand over her throat, fit his fingers into the pattern of the bruises in the same manner Filip had hours ago.

"You're very perceptive, Toriago."

His next move was unexpected. He stood and went looking for his cigarettes. Finding them, he lit one and blew smoke toward the ceiling.

He was supposed to smoke afterwards. But then nothing about Toriago seemed to fit into Bonnie's mold.

"What do you want me to do? Do you like to watch? Should I touch myself?"

More smoke. He was now leaning against the wall. What was he waiting for?

"Do you like that? Does it get you off?"

At the moment she would just as soon it was his hands that sent her over the edge, his fingers moving between her legs.

She raised her hand, was about to cup one of her breasts.

"Don't."

She stopped. "Is there something else you want? Something else you'd like me to do?"

"You can close your eyes."

"All right." She did what he asked. "Now what?"

"Now go to sleep."

Her eyes blinked open. "Sleep? You want me to go to sleep?"

"It's been a long day. For both of us. I'll see you in the morning."

Stunned, Allegra watched him step out of his black pants, flash her his tight, amazing ass, and pull on his jeans. Leaving them unzipped, his body still throbbing for release, he grabbed his shirt and jacket, then walked out of the room and closed the door.

It went without saying that if he allowed Stillman to walk over him, then maybe he wasn't the man he used to be. That just maybe he should be retired.

Doubt had been chewing Merrick up all day, and it made him feel older than ever before.

He needed a drink, but he didn't open the drawer and reach for the scotch. Instead he reached for the phone on the second ring.

To his surprise it was Sarah Finny, the woman he couldn't love until his life made sense again.

"Hello, Sarah."

"Adolf. I…haven't heard from you in several days. Is everything all right?"

"Yes. I've been busy is all. The office has been a little crazy this week."

"Okay, well… It's your birthday today, right? I was wondering if you'd like to come over for dinner?"

Merrick glanced at the calendar on his desk. He'd been so busy he'd forgotten what day it was. No wonder he'd been feeling so damn old all day.

The date sparked an old memory. If Johanna was alive she would be shopping for his favorite foods today, and when he got home she would have met him at the door with a glass of wine, and that sexy smile of hers. There would be candles burning over the fireplace, and after dinner—

"Adolf, will you come to dinner?"

"Ah…no, Sarah, I can't. I've made other plans."

"Oh. I know I should have called sooner."

"No, it's all right."

"Well, happy birthday, then, and… I'll see you when I see you."

"Thanks for the call."

Merrick hung up the phone. He should never have started seeing Sarah this past year. He'd led her to believe that he was ready for a relationship when that wasn't the case.

Not that he didn't want a normal life. Maybe after he'd caught the Chameleon and sent him to hell, he'd be able to move forward. But for now he was carrying around too much baggage. Baggage Sarah didn't need in her normal, very routine, safe life.

God willing, by this time next year he would be able to shed his old skin and be the man Sarah needed, but for now he wasn't that man. He might feel old, but he was still determined to stay in the game.

Stillman was wrong. He wasn't ready to retire. Not until he had the Chameleon on his knees begging for his life just before he killed him.

Merrick left his office well after six. He drove his black Corvette by Sarah's flower shop just as she was turning off the lights. He parked his car and watched her lock up, then watched her punch in the security code that would allow her to enter her apartment on the second floor.

He studied her shapely curves, her pretty face. She was a beautiful woman. A woman who lived an uncomplicated life. It was true she'd had her share of heartache. Her father and mother were dead, but they had died from illness, not at the hands of some maniac.

He didn't have the right to dump his messy life into her lap. Sarah deserved a man with a normal eight-to-five job, with a hobby.

No, he couldn't chance the Chameleon striking out at him through another innocent woman. He wouldn't jeopardize Sarah the way he had unknowingly gambled with Johanna's life.

Johanna.

He needed a drink. One drink to celebrate fifty-two. He deserved it. Hell, he'd been clean for six months.

One drink. Just one.

Merrick started the car and headed for the closest bar. He parked, and opened the door, then just as quickly, slammed it shut.

What was he doing? This wasn't the answer.

An hour later Merrick entered an AA meeting already in progress and slipped into the back row. He listened to the speaker, not hearing much of it, and when the meeting ended, he went home with his belly growling from hunger.

He was unlocking the outside door when a stray cat appeared on the stoop. He opened the door and the cat ran inside.

"Looking for something to eat, are you? That makes two of us."

The tabby meowed, and as Merrick headed into the elevator, the scruffy feline followed.

Like gum on his shoes, the cat stuck to him as he left the elevator and headed to his apartment. When he opened the door, the cat didn't wait for an invitation.

He opened two cans of tuna fish. Gave one to the cat and ate the other himself. He topped it off with a peanut butter sandwich, then took a shower and climbed into bed.

He laid awake for hours, his thoughts shifting from Ash Kelly to the Chameleon. But eventually, as always happened when he was about to fall asleep, Johanna's beautiful face surfaced.

Merrick fell asleep thinking about the last birthday he'd shared with his wife, his thirty-fifth. It seemed like a lifetime ago, and at the same time, only yesterday. Everything was so damn vivid, he could even feel Johanna next to him, touching him and calling out to him.

Calling out to him from the grave.

He felt himself pulse to life and he wrapped his hand around himself and envisioned that Johanna was the one stroking him, stroking him like she used to do.

It didn't take long before he was groaning and dreaming—sleeping with her ghost like he did every night.

A ghost that was determined to stay with him throughout eternity.

The next morning he awoke to find the orange tabby spooned against him, purring loudly. He reached out and stroked the cat's head.

Johanna had always wanted a cat.

"Okay," he said, "you can stay. Just don't expect too much. I'm not here much."

The cat raised her head as if she understood what he'd said, then she closed her eyes and snuggled deeper into the blankets.

It was while Merrick was getting dressed for work

that he got the call. He listened carefully to what Sly had to say, all the while wondering how Burgess Stillman could have gotten his hands on that kind of information.

He asked, "Did Ash tell you who he really is?"

"Yes. Marco Toriago."

"You said Ash is in Budapest to recover a stolen disk. What's that about?"

"It's got to do with SDECE access codes. I'm set up for communication. I'll keep you updated."

"This agent Stillman wants Ash to run down, you're sure he said it was Grant?"

"Yes."

"It looks like Stillman's problems are bigger than I thought," Merrick said. "Internal chaos. Public scrutiny and professional ruin. He's facing it all. I sympathize, but I can't condone how he's handled it."

"What are you going to do?"

"The first thing I'm going to do is find out how Stillman got his hands on Ash's identity."

Merrick hung up the phone and immediately called the airport, then headed to headquarters. He didn't go to his office. Instead, he paid a visit to Peter Briggs in the Green Room.

"Hello, Peter."

His old comrade turned his wheelchair away from his desk when he heard his name.

"If you're here about Burgess Stillman, I'm afraid he doesn't have any skeletons that I can find. But I did manage to hijack this." Peter reached for a file on his desk and handed it to Merrick. "Don't know if it'll help, but I thought it was worth looking at."

Merrick took the file, glanced at Peter's body. Since he'd lost his legs, his life had been cemented in that damn wheelchair.

Merrick had been the one who had pulled him from the carnage. Peter had spent close to a year in the hospital and when he'd finally gotten out he'd learned his wife had filed for a divorce and was about to remarry.

Merrick opened the file. It was a log of Stillman's field reports for the past six months.

"I noticed there's a lot of data missing. He's either a lousy bookkeeper, or he's hiding something."

Merrick tucked the file under his arm. "Thanks, Peter."

"You're looking good. I'm glad you pulled through your brain surgery. We should go for drinks sometime and catch up."

"I don't drink anymore. But, yeah, when I get back we'll hook up for dinner."

"Where are you going?"

"Out of town on business for a few days. Have we had any security breaches lately?"

"No. I would be the first to know."

Merrick nodded. "I'll give you a call when I get back. We'll get together."

"Sure thing."

When Merrick left he went straight back to his apartment and packed a small bag. As he zipped it shut the cat jumped up on his bed.

Damn. What to do with the cat?

With the clock ticking, he found himself calling the one person he knew who would help him in a pinch.

"Hello, Sarah."

"Adolf?"

"It's me. I have to go out of town for a while. I have a favor to ask you."

"The answer is yes. I'll see to it that Johanna gets her roses on Saturday."

"Thank you. I would appreciate that. There's one more thing. Can you come over while I'm gone and feed my cat?"

"You have a cat?"

"It recently adopted me. So can you? Can you come to the apartment and feed her while I'm away? Oh, and could you buy a litter box, too?"

"All right. What's her name?"

"Name?"

"The cat's name? What did you name her?"

"I didn't."

"She has to have a name."

"You name her."

"Me?"

"Why not? Name her whatever you want."

"I'll need a key."

"I'll drop one by." Merrick hung on the line.

"Is there something else, Adolf?"

"Ah… I really appreciate you being a good…friend. Thank you, Sarah."

"You know I'm always happy to help out any way I can. Friends do that, Adolf."

"Ah, yeah, friends. I'll see you soon."

Merrick headed to the flower shop to drop off his spare key and some money for cat food and a litter box. He thanked Sarah again, noticing that her pretty lips were glossy and that she was wearing her hair twisted up in a sexy knot.

It was late afternoon when he flew out of the airport. He settled into his seat to get some rest but found himself too anxious to sleep. As much as he understood Burgess Stillman's predicament, he wouldn't allow him to manipulate Onyxx to clean up his own mess.

And if anything happened to Ash, Stillman was going to burn in hell. In fact, he would light the match himself.

He went over Stillman's log. The first time he missed it, but on the second pass through, he found the skeleton he was hoping for.

"Shame on you, Stillman. You should have known better."

"It's good to hear from you, Filip. Are you in Budapest?"

"Yes. We got in yesterday."

"And did you make contact with Salavich?"

The Chameleon stood on the tower balcony, smoking one of his favorite Cuban cigars. The sun was up and the sky was as blue as the sea. He was enjoying the morning, anticipating another victory.

"No. We were ambushed before we got there and I was shot."

"But alive. I hope for your sake, Nightingale is also alive?"

"Yes. You never mentioned she was being followed."

"I don't believe that she is."

"Then maybe Salavich has decided to double-cross you."

"It's a possibility, but unlikely. He's being paid well for his talent in the past. And these days he is always in need of money."

"You don't have a price on my head, do you?"

"Of course not. At the moment you're the key to my next victory. That would be reckless of me. Besides, I promised you a future, Filip."

"I need time to get back on my feet before this can go forward."

"How much time?"

"A week."

"You have four days."

"And when do I get my money?"

"Once I have the decoded data, you will put Nightingale on a plane bound for Athens. When she's in the air, headed back to me, I'll transfer twenty million dollars into your Austrian account. I'll be in touch."

The Chameleon hung up the phone. A surprise ambush. He didn't like the sound of that. Or the fact that he'd been forced to deal with Filip after Yurii's unfortunate death. There were reasons why Filip had always come in second behind his brother.

"Am I interrupting?"

The Chameleon turned. "What is it, Barinski?"

"I thought you would like to know that Nightingale checked in. She wanted to know what your instructions are. She sounded a bit anxious. She said Nescosto was destroyed and that she's in Budapest with Filip. That he's been shot, but alive."

"Old news."

"She wants to know what your orders are. She's going to call back."

The Chameleon puffed on his cigar. "When she calls again, tell her she's exactly where she's supposed to be. Tell her to be patient."

Barinski nodded, but didn't leave.

"Is there something else?"

"Her sonar chip is registering some irregular vibrations."

"What does that mean?"

Barinski shoved his black-rimmed glasses up on his forehead. "It's her progesterone level."

"What about it?"

"It's elevated."

"What does that mean?"

"It means…ah… It means she's…"

"Out with it."

"It means she's horny, and perhaps doing something about it."

"She's what?"

"She's aroused."

"How the hell could that happen? Petrov is gay."

"I don't know."

The Chameleon swore. "Stay on top of it."

"Sir?"

"You know what I mean. Keep an eye on her… levels." When Barinski didn't leave, the Chameleon asked, "Now what?"

It looked as if Barinski was chewing on his thoughts and they had gotten stuck in his throat.

"Spit it out. What else don't I want to hear?"

"It's about Melita."

"Now that's a cheery subject. What about my daughter?"

"I was wondering if I could ask her to dinner?"

The question was as unexpected as it was ridiculous. The Chameleon studied Barinski's Frankenstein face to see if he was serious.

He was.

The man wanted to spend an evening with his beautiful daughter. Did he plan on wearing a bag on his head? The combination of food and Barinski's puke face would make anyone lose their appetite.

"Horny, too, Barinski?"

"No. Never. Well, not never, just… As friends. It gets lonely here on the island eating alone night after night."

Friends. The Chameleon thought a moment. Melita could use a friend. A friend she could confide in. A friend who was loyal to him. There could be nothing else, of course. He didn't need to worry about Melita's progesterone levels around Barinski. He could turn a lizard inside out.

"Why not? You have my permission to ask her to dinner. A friendship would be good for her."

Barinski left smiling—that goofy clown smile that could make a toad vomit. When he was gone, the Chameleon's thoughts returned to Nightingale. He couldn't afford to let anything to go wrong at this late date. There had already been too many setbacks.

A surprise ambush, progesterone levels… What the hell next?

He called Filip back, and asked him some pointed questions.

"I'm not screwing her if that's what you're asking. My guess is she's banging Toriago."

Toriago…

A few more questions, and the Chameleon was sitting down, listening with a curious ear, wearing a frown.

"So he saved your ass when you were ambushed?"

"That's about it."

"Not quite. Now it appears he's interested in someone else's ass, and I own that ass. Get Nightingale out of that hotel, and back on track."

When the Chameleon hung up the phone, he turned to look out the window. He saw Melita on the rocky path that led down to the shore. She was playing with those damn goats again.

For almost a year he'd kept the truth about Simon from her. She wasn't going to take the news well when she found out the fate of her brother. But as he'd told her, Simon had made his choice, as she had made hers.

There was really no need to tell her yet. She wasn't going anywhere. And there would be no surprise visit from her brother. Not ever.

Simon was dead.

Chapter 7

"Ash? Did you hear me? I said, Jazmin Grant was missing for three months the first time."

"The first time?"

Ash blinked out of his fog. He'd risen early, had left his suite while Filip and Allegra were still asleep, and had taken the elevator down to Sly's room.

"That's right. The first time she went missing was six months ago, and she was gone three months. Stillman's report claims she was taken hostage on assignment. Then suddenly she was back at the SDECE, but there's no mention of how they were able to recover her, or who had captured her. Two weeks after she returned she disappeared again. Only this time, she vanished for good. I was able to find this out by tapping into Felton Chanler's computer. That's a little strange, too. He was keeping an in-depth file on her outside the agency."

"That's odd."

"I agree. He had this, too." Sly handed Ash a photocopied picture. "I recognize the Cathedral. It's in Munich."

Ash stared at the picture of Jazmin Grant seated on a bench. There was a man with his back to the camera walking away from her. "Who is that?"

"Your guess is as good as mine."

"I wonder if Stillman knows about it?" Ash mused out loud.

"I doubt it. It's part of Chanler's private collection."

"Stillman said he wasn't sure who she was working for. I wish we could identify that guy."

Sly handed Ash more data he'd collected. Ash thumbed through it. "Where's the medical report? They should have done a medical profile on her after she returned to the SDECE. At Onyxx we're run through the wringer."

Sly leaned back in the desk chair and stacked his hands behind his head. "There's no record of her ever being hospitalized for physical or emotional analysis. If she was, those records were buried, or destroyed."

Ash sat down on the couch. "Why would Stillman put her back in the line-up only a week after she returned?"

"Good question."

"If he was negligent, that would explain why he went to Merrick under the radar with that story about Chanler and Grant dying at Nescosto." Ash continued to read the data Sly had lifted. When he picked up the picture again, he said, "She's wearing a trench coat."

"Yeah, I noticed."

Ash glanced out the window, feeling exhausted and frustrated. He hadn't slept all night. In fact he'd spent half the night in the bar. No, he hadn't ordered a drink, though Naldo had had a few too many—his excuse, he was drinking for both of them, as well as bragging about getting a hotel maid in the shower with him.

At least someone had gotten some action.

He'd gone back up to his suite around three in the morning. He'd checked in on Petrov, then had slipped into his bedroom. Allegra was sleeping on her side, and he'd stood there and watched her for close to a half hour.

"You all right?"

Ash sat forward and tossed the data on the coffee table. "I didn't sleep much last night."

"Anything in particular keeping you awake?"

Ash pulled his phone from his pocket. "I've got an automatic record on this phone Stillman gave me. Listen to this."

He punched a button on his phone panel and Allegra's voice filled the room. "This is Nightingale. Yurii's dead, and Filip and I are in Budapest. I need instructions. I'll call back. Don't call this number."

Sly dropped his hands from behind his head and sat up. "Allegra?"

"It's her."

"Did you trace the call?"

"I tried. Whoever received it must be able to block any attempt to trace." Ash let out a frustrated sigh and reached for his cigarettes. "Dammit, I wish I knew what the hell was going on."

He stood and started to pace.

"How did she get your phone?"

Ash took a drag off his cigarette. He didn't want to mention what happened after he'd showered and entered the bedroom last night, but Sly was there to help, and he couldn't do that blindfolded.

"Last night while Filip was asleep she came into my bedroom. I keep my phone in my jacket pocket. She used the phone while I was in the shower. When I came into the bedroom she was there."

"And how did you know she had used the phone?"

"I didn't at first. Then she made a move on me. I…countered it." Ash shook his head. "She's a beautiful woman. I've been out of circulation for a year. I—"

"You don't have to explain it. I've seen her."

"I thought, what the hell. One night, right? I went to my jacket, took my phone out to shut it off. I had told Naldo to check in before he turned in for the night." Ash looked up. "I didn't want anyone interrupting us. That's when I noticed the phone was in the left pocket. I always keep it in the right. I noticed the record button was lit up and I knew someone had used my phone."

"Did you sleep with her? Sorry, you don't have to answer that."

Ash sat back down. "No. But I would have."

"And she was willing because she was determined to cover her tracks."

"Looks that way."

"A woman who makes sacrifices."

"Thanks. That makes me feel better."

"I didn't mean that the way it sounded."

"It's okay. I've already went over all the angles. Whoever she's working for, she's used to giving her all."

Sly grinned. "Loyalty is an admirable trait."

"Ain't it though."

"Maybe you should play her game. If she's still willing, get her back in the bedroom. Two can play that game."

"You're joking, right?"

"We need to know who she is. Get me a fingerprint, DNA, something I can run with."

Ash considered Sly's suggestion. "Okay. I'll get you what you need. But I'll do it my way."

When he left Sly's suite, he headed back to his own room. When he stepped inside he heard the shower running. He looked in on Filip and found him still sleeping. That explained who was in the shower.

He stepped out on the balcony, smoked another cigarette. Fifteen minutes later he stepped back into the living room to call Casso Salavich to reschedule their meeting, but a knock at the door interrupted him.

With his gun in his pocket, he answered the door. To his surprise, it was Salavich and six bodyguards.

"Casso Salavich, Mr. Toriago. I don't blame you for avoiding Ballvaro after what happened yesterday, so I've come to you."

That Salavich had taken the first step was a good sign. "Did you find yesterday's shooter?" Ash asked.

"Not yet. But my men are still looking. We will find him, and before he dies, we will know who he was working for."

Ash didn't correct him on the gender mistake. He still believed it was Grant. He was glad to hear that Salavich hadn't found her. He needed her alive, and it sounded as if that wasn't part of Salavich's agenda.

"Are you going to invite us in, Mr. Toriago?"

Ash stepped aside to allow Salavich to enter. Three guards remained in the hall, and three followed Salavich inside—all of them big brutes with football shoulders, thick sideburns, and size twenty shoes.

Ash walked back into the living room. "Can I get you something, Señor Salavich?"

"Nothing, thank you."

One of the brutes lifted Salavich's coat from his shoulders and the bald-headed don walked into the suite as if he owned stock in the hotel, which he well might.

"So, Mr. Toriago, we will sit and discuss the particulars of your new venture, and what I can do for you."

Ash played it cool. He kept his face stone serious, the face of a man who was used to dealing with disreputable criminals.

Although Stillman thought Ash was a shoe-in to entice Salavich into a partnership as Marco Toriago, his family had been out of circulation a long time. His father might have left a legacy behind, but his son had been tagged a wild renegade with too much money and too much libido.

The question Salavich would be asking himself today was if Marco Toriago had tamed his reckless nature and was following in his father's cunning footsteps, or if there was a weakness in the bloodline.

Salavich made himself comfortable on a stuffed

chair. He wore a shiny suit worth over two grand, and a gold chain around his thick neck. He was a fat man, whose obvious passion had become excess. No doubt gluttony would kill him before a bullet.

He glanced around Ash's suite.

"Nice place."

"It'll do, but I prefer home."

"And where is home these days?"

"Villahermosa." It was true. His family still owned a home in Mexico. A little hacienda where he could hide away from the world a few weeks out of the year. After this, he would no doubt have to sell it.

Ash relaxed on the couch, reached for his cigarettes, and lit up.

"Explain this business deal you think I would be interested in, Mr. Toriago. I must tell you I rarely do business with someone younger than me. Experience breeds longevity. So you'll have to convince me that your father's wisdom is hereditary."

Bingo.

Ash blew smoke. "I'm not here to sell myself. I have merchandise and I'm looking for a distributor. If you aren't interested, I can find someone who will be."

"We all must sell ourselves, Mr. Toriago. As I recall mistakes were made years ago. Critical mistakes that sent you to prison. Your father killed himself there. My condolences on his passing, but you can see my problem."

How his father had died was not something Ash wanted to remember, although he had lived with the guilt of it since. Being penned up in a Mexican prison had been humiliating for Estabon. Stripped and flogged day after day had been too much for a proud man. He'd succumbed to the humiliation, a humiliation Estabon chose to check out of one night after six months of broken pride and disgrace.

His body was found the next morning hanging from a pipe in his cell.

"I'm curious why after so many years you've decided to go back into business."

"I was never out of business. Just clearing the way. Litigation can take time."

That brought a smile to Salavich's face. "Let's talk merchandise and money."

Ash took a drag off his cigarette. Blowing more smoke. "Ice. A billion to start. A shipment each month after that."

"That's quite a promise. Of course, I'll need proof of quality, and that you will be able to sustain such a commitment."

"That won't be a problem. Of course, I'll need to ease my mind as well."

"Meaning?"

"I'm told you're the man here in Europe. But if you can't find one lone shooter, it makes me wonder if that's simply a rumor."

"You push hard, Toriago. Filip Petrov was my friend. He did not deserve to die yesterday. I will find his killer."

"Then if and when you settle this shooter business, we'll get down to settling ours. It would be reckless of me to get caught in the cross fire of an old war with Petrov's enemies when it has nothing to do with what I'm about."

"A wise decision. We will earn each others' trust, and go from there. Going into business with someone is much like climbing into bed with a woman. Talk is cheap, the action speaks volumes. Come to dinner tonight at Ballvaro."

"I can't. I'm babysitting an under-the-weather friend."

"I wasn't aware you had friends in Budapest."

"Actually he is a friend of yours, too."

"This friend. Does he have a name?"

"Filip Petrov."

"Filip is here? I thought you said he was dead?"

"No, you said that. He survived yesterday with my help."

"That is good news!"

"He was shot. But he's alive."

"Where can I reach him?"

"He's here."

"Here?"

Ash glanced up to see Allegra lingering in the hall. She was staring at Salavich. He glanced at her, but he made sure he didn't show her too much interest. He was under a microscope at the moment and a wrong move could put him out in the cold before he got through Salavich's front door.

It was obvious that she'd been eavesdropping on the conversation. He asked, "Is Filip awake?"

"Yes."

Casso turned, saw Allegra and immediately stood. "I would like to see him."

"He's battling a high fever at the moment. I don't think he's up to company."

"He'll want to see me, my dear. You are?"

"Allegra."

Casso made eye contact with Ash. "Your woman is lovely, Mr. Toriago."

"She's not my woman." Ash offered her a flat smile. "She's Filip's…playmate."

Salavich stood and crossed the room to where Allegra stood. He reached for her hand and brought it to his lips. Kissing it, he said, "Casso Salavich, Miss…"

"Nightingale. Allegra Nightingale."

"Nightingale… Yes, I seem to remember him mentioning your name. Yesterday's ambush at Ballvaro was unfortunate, my dear, but rest assured I will find those responsible. Now, what can I do to help Filip?"

She glanced at Ash as if she expected him to intervene. He stubbed out his cigarette and came to his feet.

"Do you have a private physician, Señor Salavich?"

By evening, Filip was on his feet. Salavich's doctor had pumped him full of antibiotics and put his arm in a sling.

He had informed Allegra that they were going back to Ballvaro. She didn't ask why, she was simply too anxious to leave. She couldn't concentrate with Toriago so close by. She kept remembering how he had touched her and then how quickly he'd backed off.

She heard a knock on the door, heard Filip speaking.

When the bedroom door opened she expected it to be Filip. But it was Toriago.

"Salavich's car is here."

"Where's Filip?"

"In the hall speaking to one of Salavich's men. Are you ready to go?"

"More than ready."

He gave her a grin, stepped inside and closed the door. "It's not too late."

"Too late for what?"

"I can still get you out of here, but that's not what you want, is it?"

"I don't know what you're talking about."

Allegra picked up her bag, but when she tried to move past him to the door he reached out and took her arm and stopped her. "Would you like to use my phone again before you leave?"

She jerked away from him, a warning bell going off inside her head.

He pulled his phone from his pocket, punched a button, and suddenly her voice was filling the room.

She made a dive for the phone, afraid that Filip would hear it. "Shut it off," she demanded.

He flattened her against the door and held her there. With the phone out of her reach, he turned down the volume, but her words continued to damn her.

When it was over, he said, "Okay, Miss Nightingale, what's the game? What were your instructions before Yurii died, and what are you doing in Budapest with Filip?"

"None of this involves you. Forget you have that and forget me."

He leaned in, his mouth inches from hers. "Tell me the truth and the debt you still owe me is gone."

"I paid my debt last night. It was your choice to take as much or as little as you wanted. If you feel cheated today that's your fault, not mine. Now do I scream, or are you going to back off?"

"Scream and I take this to Filip. I wonder what he'd think? What he would do? Maybe this time he'd snap your neck instead of just marking it up."

"Allegra, the car is waiting."

Filip's voice boomed from the living room.

"Forget you have that. My business won't alter your plans with Salavich. Just walk away."

"I wish I could." He leaned in and kissed her then, a breathy memory of what they'd shared the night before.

"Allegra! I'm waiting."

When he stepped back, he said, "I'll see you soon."

"Please stay away from me."

"Not on your life."

She walked into the hall, and he didn't try to stop her. Allegra concentrated on getting her breathing under control, but she knew she'd failed the minute Filip laid eyes on her.

Ash followed her down the hall, after tucking his phone in his pocket. Filip was standing by the couch in the living room, and he looked like he was in a sour mood. Either that, or in a lot of pain.

After he ordered Allegra to the car, he pulled out his wallet and handed Ash a thousand dollars. "I know that saving a life is priceless, but at least that will cover the new clothes on my back, and Allegra's as well. Goodbye, Toriago."

"The shooter is still out there. Watch your back."

Filip had started to walk away. He stopped and offered Ash a nod. "You, too, Toriago. We are both in a dangerous business. We never know when our time is up."

Ash followed Filip to the door. As Petrov stepped out and started down the corridor, Salavich's guard handed Ash an envelope.

"There is a party at Ballvaro in a few days. Mr. Salavich wants to extend an invitation. He hopes you will accept."

Ash closed the door, then ripped open the envelope. It was an invitation to Casso's daughter's birthday party in three days. He smiled, then started to make plans.

Chapter 8

The beating had come out of nowhere. At least that's what she had thought at the moment it was happening, but she knew different now.

They had cruised through the iron gate at Ballvaro three days ago, had been introduced to Casso Salavich's wife, Sophia, and his daughter Dominika, and then they had been shown to their rooms on the second floor.

She had just taken off her coat when Filip had come at her. He had shoved her down on the bed, and with no explanation, or warning, he'd punched her in the stomach and knocked the wind out of her. While she was gasping for air, he'd proceeded to hit her, over and over again, calling her everything from a slut to a whore. He hadn't stopped until she couldn't move.

It was a good thing that Ballvaro was a huge estate and that she wasn't required to make appearances. She hadn't been able to get out of bed until this morning, and even now she walked slow and carefully, as if she was walking on a carpet of broken glass instead of an inch thick of plush.

Filip had been careful were he'd landed each calculated punch. No one would be able to see any bruises, not unless she was stripped naked.

She'd called Cyrus again—she'd snuck into Salavich's office to use the phone—and he'd told her that she was to stay in Budapest with Filip. Once he'd said that, she'd decided not to tell him about the beating. After all, she was a deep cover agent, and life in the trenches wasn't all sugar and cream. This was her first mission for him, and she needed to stay strong to prove herself.

There had been no explanation until last night why Filip had beaten her. But the words *slut* and *whore* had given her a clue. Toriago must have told him about what had happened between them in his hotel suite.

The strange thing that she couldn't explain was the dream she'd had last night. It was as if the beating had jarred a piece of forgotten memory loose and she'd dreamt about being strapped in a chair and interrogated.

This morning she'd had another flash of memory. She'd been scaling a tall building, but when she reached the top someone was there cutting the rope. Since then there were more scenarios—a dozen old movies playing inside her head all at once—old spy movies, and she was the star.

We fly no flag. Our responsibility is to the world and to those who can't protect themselves. Our commission is of the highest secrecy. You've been chosen to join the team. This location will remain inaccessible to you for a good reason.

You've been chosen.

Highest security.

We fly no flag...

Allegra dressed in her jeans and a sweater. As she left her room, she pulled on her coat. She had the freedom to come and go, and she slipped out of the bastion into the crisp morning air.

She walked down the shoveled paths and let the sun warm her face. Like the good spy she was, she counted the guards and paid special attention to where they were stationed on the property. There were surveillance cameras, too. No doubt someone was watching her at this very minute.

It was still early when she returned to the house. She went back up to her room. It was the first long walk she'd taken since the beating. She knew she'd feel weak, but she needed to regain her strength.

She stood at the window, looked over Ballvaro once again, from a different vantage point. The old Hungarian castle had at least four dozen rooms on three levels, with private bathrooms in every bedroom, two elegant dining rooms, and a grand ballroom. There was a helicopter pad out back, and every exit had at least two guards posted.

But that wasn't all that made Casso's bastion so eye-catching. For those without a suspicious mind, there was plenty of entertainment. An indoor courtyard overlooking the river, with a sophisticated electronic system that provided artificial sunshine to support a swimming pool, an array of tropical vegetation, and more flowers than the inside of a greenhouse. But there were more lavish amusements—a workout room, which it was obvious Casso never used, a music room, and three wine cellars.

From the moment she and Filip had arrived, the house had been in a redecorating frenzy. Salavich's daughter was turning eighteen and tonight they would celebrate the event with a birthday party fit for a princess.

It was odd. Even knowing who and what Salavich was, she couldn't help but like Sophia and Dominika. They were ordinary women caught up in an evil world.

She hadn't seen Filip much since they'd arrived. He spent most of his time behind closed doors in Salavich's study. She had been given her own room, a beautiful suite decorated in peach and muted greens. It was across the hall from Filip's room—the reason given was so that he could rest more comfortably while he recovered.

That was ironic. He'd spent very little time there, while she had been the one recovering from injuries.

She left the window and entered the bathroom. She had just stepped out of the shower when she heard her door open. When she stepped back into the bedroom, Filip was sitting on her bed.

"We need to talk. I've ordered breakfast. It'll be served in my room. I'll explain then. Fifteen minutes. Don't dress. Come in your robe."

He left without another word, or an explanation.

Allegra glanced at the clock. Fifteen minutes. Breakfast, a little talking, and then what? Another beating?

Come in your robe....

She waited as long as she could before she left her room. Twelve minutes later she knocked on his door, and he ordered her inside. Breakfast had already been delivered, and Filip was seated at the small table surrounded by windows.

His suite was as bright and lavish as hers. A red theme, with masculine furnishings. From the window you could see the snow glistening along the frozen shoreline and in the distance, Margaret Island and the bridge.

"Sit. I ordered for you."

"I'm not very hungry." Allegra sat, tucking the robe closer around her.

He never looked at her. He uncovered the omelet and said, "Eat it anyway."

She poured a glass of orange juice, and had just taken a sip when he asked, "While I was on my back burning up with fever what else did you do besides screw around with Toriago?"

Where was this going? She wasn't about to argue with him about the perimeters in which the words screwed around were defined. She had no wish to anger him again, and if he thought she'd slept with Toriago, then she was willing to let it ride, as long as it didn't turn him into a maniac again.

"I stayed in the room. Except for when I went out to get your medical supplies and a few pieces of clothes for us. That was it."

He sat back and studied her. "Did Toriago speak to anyone?"

"Just his chauffeur."

"No one else came to the room?"

"No."

"And when Toriago left the suite, he never said where he was going?"

"Why so much interest in Toriago?"

"Because I suddenly don't trust his motives, and I don't need an outsider screwing this up."

"Screwing what up? When are you going to tell me why we're here, and what it has to do with Salavich?"

He looked up and smiled. It was a smug secret smile, and suddenly she felt as if once she learned what they were here to do, she wasn't going to like it.

He said, "I'll tell you why we're here when you're services are needed, and not before."

He went back to eating, and she noticed he was using his arm some.

"Is that what you wanted to discuss with me? Toriago?"

"He's only part of it. Tonight is Salavich's daughter's birthday party. There will be some important people I need to meet with. While I'm busy—"

"You want me to stay here out of sight. I can do that."

"No. I need you to attend the party. I admit I feel like a fish out of water here. Casso lives like a king, with too many servants and too much clutter. This was Yurii's expertise, dressing up and going to parties. He enjoyed meeting people and sampling wine and eating silly little sandwiches." He paused, took a bite of his omelet. "Tonight you will keep up our game. Make yourself available to me when I signal you, and make yourself scarce when the topic of business comes up. Be seen, look pretty and keep your mouth shut."

"I can do that."

"I took the liberty of sending out for some clothes yesterday. Casso has people who shop for him. One of the women went shopping for you." He sat back and reached for his coffee. "After you finish eating we'll see what looks best for tonight."

He'd invited her into his room to be fitted for a party dress. Allegra's appetite returned, and she finished the omelet. When she pushed the plate away, Filip went into the bedroom, telling her to follow him.

She entered the room to find six dresses laid out on the bed, each one outfitted with matching shoes and sexy lingerie.

Casso's shoppers had good taste. But only one dress looked like her. In agreement with Filip on at least one account, she'd never been much for mingling with strangers dressed in uncomfortable clothes and shoes that she couldn't run in.

She was just starting to relax when he said, "Drop the robe so I can see which dress will hide your bruises."

She had chosen the black dress. It was simple and elegant, but most of all, it was the safest choice. She liked the high collar, and it hid every bruise and black-and-blue spot between her chest and her thighs.

But just when she had thought it was her choice to make, Filip had turned the tables on her and had insisted on the gold glitz with the plunging neckline and two dramatic side slits that would show off her legs with every move she made.

Squeezed into the dress, she now stood in front of the mirror wondering who was staring back at her. She didn't remember ever wearing anything so daring, or expensive. And her hair—Filip had insisted that she wear it up, so she'd fashioned a messy knot—she had done herself, the talent for it coming out of nowhere, just like the memories that had been haunting her today.

She finished putting on an extra layer of makeup, then willed a piece of Bonnie's wisdom to surface and settle her nerves. But what popped into her head instead was a pair of hands stroking her body, and a pair of lips stealing her breath.

Toriago…

Why she couldn't put him out of her mind, she didn't know. But the memory of how he'd touched her wouldn't leave her. It was as if he'd crawled inside her head, and his hands had branded her skin.

She glanced at the ornate clock on the dresser. It was almost show time. And she would be showing a lot this evening. But luckily none of the bruises.

She heard a hard rap at the door, then it opened.

"Are you ready?"

"Coming."

She walked through the bedroom door to find Filip standing in a tux. She was used to seeing him in jeans, his dark hair long and wild. But tonight he was dressed all in black, his hair pulled back to expose his square jaw and prominent nose.

"You look like one of Casso's mistresses."

Filip's words jarred her out of her musing. "One of Casso's mistresses?"

"Don't look so surprised. Every man has at least one."

"Do you?"

"I told you, I have no need for a woman. Come here."

Allegra crossed the room. He pulled a gold garter from his pocket and then knelt on one knee.

"Lift your right foot and put it on my knee."

Allegra did what he said, and he slipped the sexy garter over her foot and worked it past her knee. His fingers settled the garter high on her left thigh, then he pulled a Walther .22 from his pocket and strapped it beneath the garter.

"There. Just in case there's trouble."

"Do you think there will be?"

"There's a large guest list, and we still don't know who ambushed our car." He stood and opened the door. "Shall we go?"

She heard the music coming from downstairs. She stepped into the hall. When they reached the staircase, she looked down at the wall-to-wall people below.

When they descended the stairs, Casso Salavich turned away from a guest to greet them, but Allegra barely heard what he said to them. She was too surprised to see that Toriago was the man Salavich had been speaking to.

He looked as handsome and dangerous as ever, and she was fully aware that her heart was racing. She told herself it was a mistake, all of it, but the memory was there, and no matter how hard she tried, it hadn't dimmed.

"Again, Filip, I commend you on your taste," Casso said. "Allegra, you look magnificent. What do you say, Mr. Toriago?"

"I'd say Filip is a lucky man. *Buenas tardes, señorita*. It's good to see you again."

Toriago's eyes held Allegra's a few seconds longer, then Filip stretched out his hand and Toriago shook it.

"Toriago. I'm surprised to see you here."

"I invited him," Salavich said. "Toriago and I are discussing a business venture."

She felt Toriago's eyes on her, drifting over the thin straps that kept her breasts in constant danger of double jeopardy, then over her flat stomach and narrow hips.

The dress was wicked and revealed too much. Why Filip had chosen it, she would never know. All evening she would be aware of just how little she had on. Her senses would be heightened and her guard high.

Perhaps that was it.

"Come, Filip, I want to introduce you to someone. Toriago, you don't mind entertaining the lovely Allegra, do you?"

"I'd be honored. That is, if Filip trusts me."

Filip's smile never wavered. "With my life, Toriago. Surely with my woman's as well."

No, Allegra thought. She didn't want to be left alone with Toriago. A wrong move, a wrong look and after the party Filip would be waiting for her behind her bedroom door ready to pounce. She wasn't healed enough to withstand another attack.

But it was too late. Filip was already lowering his head and kissing her cheek as if they were truly a couple. A final nod to Toriago and he was striding off with Salavich.

It was hard to believe that she could look more beautiful than she had at the hotel. The private thought should have been the furthest thing from Ash's mind, but it was there, along with several other thoughts that had nagged him for the past three days.

He'd been busy since she and Filip had left his suite at the hotel. He'd dug deep to find out everything he could about her, but in the end what he'd learned was even more a puzzlement—Allegra Nightingale didn't exist.

But everyone was from somewhere. So who the hell was she, and where did she come from—this woman who didn't exist on paper anywhere in the world?

Ash took her hand and tugged her down the last two steps. Not letting go, he said, "So, Miss Nightingale, you never mentioned where you and Filip met. You've got a French accent, so is that home?"

She pulled her hand away. "You're right—I never mentioned where Filip and I met, and I have a French accent."

"A little hostile this evening, are we?"

"It must be the company."

Ash grinned. "Touché, *señorita*."

His gaze drifted. She was dressed in shimmering gold, and it lit up her slender curves like a neon sign.

"I see the bruise on your neck is almost gone."

"Surprised there aren't more?"

Ash frowned. "I don't know what you mean."

"Don't you?"

"No."

"If that's the way you want to play it."

"Play what?"

"You don't have to keep me company, Toriago. I'm capable of surviving this party on my own. In fact, I'm sure I'll do better on my own."

She attempted to walk off and Ash stopped her by taking hold of her arm. "I wouldn't think of leaving you alone. Not dressed like that."

She jerked away from him. "Don't touch me."

She was overly chippy with him. He caught her glance across the room and he followed her gaze to where Filip stood in the middle of a group of men. He was listening to what was being said, but his attention was on them.

"Did something happen after you left the hotel?"

She glanced up at him. "No. Nothing that concerns you."

Ash spotted Sly sipping a glass of champagne against the wall. It hadn't been hard to get his comrade inside. The ballroom was congested—Casso's guest list had to be at least three hundred. Sly looked like just another suit in the room—overdressed and anxious for the evening to end.

Because Ash didn't know what he might be up against tonight, Sly had suggested that he be the one to nose around Salavich's bastion.

Allegra was still standing next to him at the bottom of the stairs when a couple tried to squeeze past them. It forced her into him, and Ash reached out to keep her from being knocked over. When he grabbed her, he heard her suck in a sharp breath of air—a reaction someone would make if they were in pain.

He glanced at her face and saw that she was biting her lip. "What's wrong?"

"Nothing's wrong. Now if you'll excuse me, I think I'll see if I can find a viper to play with. It will certainly be safer than talking to you."

* * *

Allegra was about to make her escape when she saw Sophia Salavich headed their way.

"Mrs. Salavich is on her way over. I suppose it would be too much to ask for you to be polite. She's nothing like her husband."

"I'll be whatever you wish, *señorita,* as long as you promise to dance with me later."

Allegra feigned a laugh. "You're joking, of course."

"Dead serious."

"No."

"Say yes, and I won't embarrass you by bringing up that sexy mole on your left breast."

She glared at him, but she knew better than to challenge him. He'd already proven that he didn't make idle threats.

"There you are, Allegra. How lovely you look tonight."

Allegra turned to Sophia, smiled. "Thank you. I wanted to tell you that you did a wonderful job decorating the house. It's beautiful."

Casso's wife was dressed in green velvet, her midnight-black hair piled high on her head. Three strands of diamonds circled her neck, and matching chandeliers clung to her ears. As far as the house went, no expense had been spared, and everywhere you looked, there were bouquets of pink roses and spider mums.

"I haven't seen Dominika yet, but she must be excited."

"She's spoilt, is what she is, but then she's an only child, and Casso is determined to give her the world."

Sophia glanced at Allegra's dress. "I'm a bit surprised with your choice. I imagined you would choose the black silk."

"Actually I favored the black, but Filip preferred the gold."

"Without seeing the black, I'm with Filip. A man doesn't always like to imagine everything."

Allegra gave Toriago a black look.

Sophia, on the other hand, was a gracious host. "We haven't met, have we?"

"No. I would have remembered if we had. Marco Toriago."

"I'm afraid that doesn't mean anything, and if that offends you, I'm sorry."

"No offense taken."

"I admit half the guests are Casso's business associates. Are you one of them?"

"A new friend."

"Oh, dear. One of my staff has just signaled me. I hope nothing's wrong. Excuse me, please." Sophia reached out and touched Allegra's hand. "Enjoy the party." She started to walk away, then stopped. "It was nice meeting you, Mr. Toriago."

Allegra didn't waste time. The minute Sophia was gone, she said, "Filip's signaling me as well. Enjoy the party, Toriago. Maybe you'll get lucky and choke on a sandwich."

When she joined Filip, he said, "Toriago looks as bored as I am tonight. What did you two talk about? A rendezvous later?"

This time she was not going to lie. If Filip didn't like what he heard maybe he should break a few of

Toriago's ribs. She said, "He asked me to dance. I told him no."

"I just learned from Casso that Toriago's trying to set up some kind of big deal. I want to know what it is."

"Then ask him."

"I think it would be better coming from you. Accept the dance, and see what you can find out."

Chapter 9

To say the ballroom looked like a pink parade was an understatement. There was pink linen on the banquet tables, and pink frosting on a giant birthday cake. Even the six-piece band that played in the far corner was wearing pink satin suits.

Sophia had thought of everything…in pink.

Allegra eyed the dancing guests. She knew how to dance, but that didn't mean she wanted to take a spin around the dance floor with Toriago.

No, she didn't want to dance, or talk to him, but Filip would want an answer by the time the party ended.

She saw Dominika sitting alone at a table, and she wondered why the birthday girl wasn't enjoying the music on the dance floor. But then she realized that only a few of the guest were her own age.

Like everything else, Dominika was dressed in party pink, a strapless gown with a full skirt that made her look like a prom queen. Suddenly the birthday girl was smiling as a man walked toward her carrying two glasses of punch.

Allegra watched as Toriago offered Dominika one of the glasses, then he pulled something out of his pocket and set it on the table in front of her. It was a small velvet box, and the gesture piqued Allegra's curiosity

She continued to watch as Dominika set her punch down on the table, picked up the gift and unwrapped it. She came to her feet quickly and wrapped her arms around Toriago's neck.

Allegra shoved away from the wall and shouldered her way through the guests. Toriago was speaking to Dominika, at the same time helping her put his gift on her wrist, when she arrived. She waited until Dominika looked up and when she did, she was beaming.

"Allegra, look, isn't it fabulous?" Suddenly Dominika thrust her arm forward. "Marco bought me a diamond bracelet." Smiling up at him like a young girl who had lost her heart for the first time, she said, "How did you know that diamonds are my favorite?"

"Yes, *Marco*. How did you know?" Allegra parroted.

"I thought they were every woman's favorite."

"Oh, I forgot to do the introductions. Allegra, this is—"

"It's okay, honey, we've met." Allegra ignored the grin on Toriago's face, and continued to give Casso's daughter her full attention. "I wanted to wish you happy birthday."

"Thank you."

Suddenly Allegra was hit by a memory.

Diamonds are forever, baby-doll. Don't ever forget that. Collect them like stamps, and remember, if you have to sleep with a snake, make sure he's a rich one.

"Allegra, did you hear me?"

She blinked. "What?"

"I said, women like diamonds because they sparkle, right?"

For a pretty girl she was terribly naive, Allegra thought.

Toriago must have read her mind. Sporting a slippery smile, he said, "Do you have some words of wisdom for Dominika on her eighteenth birthday, Allegra?"

She certainly had an opinion.

Why not, she thought. "It all goes back to Eve in the garden surrounded by snakes," she said, giving Toriago a droll smile. "It wasn't really about the fruit. Adam tempted Eve with a diamond, never realizing that he had just given her the key to her freedom."

"How?" Dominika asked.

"Diamonds are a good investment, and being the smart woman Eve was, she took the diamond knowing its value surpassed seven minutes of pleasure."

Dominika blushed. "But she did pay for it? I mean, she said yes. That's what the story is about…sinning."

Allegra leaned closer, and whispered, "It wasn't really about sinning, it was about sacrifice and independence. So my wisdom for today is make sure the sacrifice is worth the price, never work cheap and stockpile your diamonds. Oh, and one more thing. Snakes come in all shapes and sizes."

Toriago laughed out loud. It was a rich laugh, and Dominika was completely taken in by it, and him.

So much for the lesson on snakes, Allegra thought.

"I have to show Mother." Dominika suddenly kissed Toriago on the cheek. "Thank you…Marco."

Left alone with Mr. Snake, she said, "Very smooth, Toriago. You have a fan."

He shrugged. "It wasn't my intent."

"Wasn't it?"

"That was quite a story."

"Words to live by, if she's smart."

"Is that how you live?"

"It's the way I would like to live."

"What's stopping you?"

Allegra didn't answer. "I came to ask you two simple questions. Why are you here tonight, and what is your business with Salavich?"

"Are those your questions, or Filip's?"

"Does it matter?"

"Afraid I'm going to interfere with your business with Salavich?"

"You don't know what my business is."

"Exactly. I'll share with you, if you share with me. Should we go somewhere quiet and discuss it?"

He took her hand, noticed her bracelet, and brushed his thumb over the large round stone. "Gold amber." He looked up. "Not diamonds?"

He was studying the Greek inscription on the silver band when someone yelled *Toriago* from across the room. The gunshot exploded into the crowd a second later, and Marco jerked Allegra sideways, then shoved her to the floor.

Another gunshot turned the ballroom into a stampede of screaming guests as the room suddenly turned into chaos.

"Get under the table and stay there," Toriago said, then he was off and running as more shots fed the hysteria.

Allegra didn't crawl under the table. Instead she pulled her .22 from her garter. Her ribs were on fire from Toriago shoving her to the floor, but she ignored the pain and tried to keep from being stepped on as the crowd swarmed toward the exit.

She heard a woman scream, and she searched the room and saw Dominika standing in the middle of the ballroom frozen in fear.

Allegra bolted to her feet, and shoved through the crowd to reach Casso's daughter. She grabbed her by the arm, and pulled her behind the long banquet table just as a shot hit the birthday cake and sent it into a million pieces.

A fire had broken out to add to the mayhem— several candles had been knocked over in the foray, and now the linen tablecloths were on fire.

"Stay here," Allegra instructed.

"I'm afraid."

"I know. But it'll be all right. Just stay here."

Allegra saw a man dressed as a guest tucking a gun inside his jacket as he tried to get lost in the crowd. She started after him just as the lights went out.

Undeterred, she pushed her way through the crowd. There was a side door that the caterers used, and she felt her way along the wall, then slipped through it into the hallway.

Her eyes had adjusted to the darkness, and she

watched and waited as the crowd scattered once they exited the ballroom. Casso's guards were trying to usher them outside as they came through the door.

She wasn't standing there for more than a couple of minutes when she saw a man veer away from the guards and head for the courtyard.

She slipped off her shoes and hurried after him. The good news was, when she reached the garden, she saw it was lit by a dozen torch lights. But the bad news was, stopping to take off her shoes had cost her time, and she had no idea which path the gunman had taken.

She took a wild guess, and headed down the first path she came to. The courtyard was a maze of twists and turns—paths leading into private gardens, paths leading to several stone fountains.

She moved quickly, her gun out in front of her as she listened for a sound that would give her a clue as to which path the gunman had taken.

She skirted the pool, and turned down another path, then another. The garden was as dense as a jungle, with plenty of places to hide.

She had almost given up when she heard footsteps. When she realized that they were behind her, she spun around, but it was too late. The gunman had already spotted her, but he didn't shoot.

"Hell of a dress, baby. But then you would look good in rags."

Allegra recognized his voice. Unable to believe who was standing twenty feet away, she said, "Chanler, is that you?"

"It's me. Hello, Jaz. Drop the gun or I'll shoot you here and now."

"Shoot me? Why?"

"Don't play stupid. We both know you're far from it."

"Did Stillman send you?"

"No. I'm here on my own. By the way, you look good as a brunette." He stepped closer. "I see you've had some work done, too. Not a lot, but enough to fool the world. But not me, baby. Who knows you better than your old partner?

"How did you find me?"

"I just followed the stench. It's true what they say. You can smell a traitor a mile away."

Allegra frowned. "What do you mean, a traitor?"

"I tried to tell Stillman something was wrong with you when you came back to headquarters after you'd gone missing. He wouldn't listen. He just wouldn't accept that the perfect Jazmin Grant would sell out the SDECE. I'll bet he'll listen now."

"I never sold anyone out. It's not what you think, Chanler. I'm under deep cover."

He laughed. "And I'm James Bond's son."

Allegra suddenly felt light-headed. Traitor… How could Chanler ever think that she would betray the SDECE?

"I had to let Jazmin Grant die, Felton. I had to take a new name and a new face. But I'm no traitor. You have to believe me."

"Tell it to Stillman. I'm taking you back."

"No. I can't go with you. I'm in the middle of a mission and I can't walk away."

"You'll walk, or I'll carry you out. Choose, Jaz. Dead or alive, you're leaving with me."

* * *

Burgess Stillman left the corner cafe in the heart of Paris unaware that he was being watched. He walked slowly to the car that idled along the curb, and as he opened a rear door, Merrick left the alley.

He wore his disguise well—dressed poorly, and walking like he'd been plagued with a back ailment most of his life, he shoved his gun into Stillman's face the minute he climbed into the car.

"Slide over," he demanded, "slowly."

"What the—?"

"I said slide over." Merrick had taken on a French accent, and he sounded as desperate as he looked.

Stillman moved over and Merrick climbed in. Closing the door, he said, "Tell your driver to leave his phone and gun on the dash and get out of the car."

"Do what he says, Louis."

"But, sir—"

"Do it. He's armed."

"*Oui*, Louis, I've got a gun pointed at your boss. Go stand under that lamp post, and put your hands around the post. Hug it good, hands together."

Stillman's driver opened his door and climbed out. He walked to the lamp post and hugged it like he was told. Inside the car, Merrick pulled off his black stocking cap and revealed himself to Burgess Stillman.

"Merrick. You bastard, what the hell do you think you're doing?"

"That's a good question, Stillman. That's what I would like you to explain to me. How did you find out Ash Kelly's real identity? I want a name."

"He's been in contact with you?"

"No. I made contact with him."

"How did you know where to find him?"

Merrick grinned. "How do you think?"

"You had him followed."

"As you said in my office two weeks ago, whatever works. Blackmail, or just a little innocent deception. It's all part of the game, no?" Merrick's smile didn't reach his eyes. "The name of your informant, or I'll kill you here and now."

"That's extreme. It would ruin you for sure. You and Onyxx."

"I'm in Washington right now. Your death will be reported as a random robbery by a desperate thief."

"You're crazy, *mon ami*. You can't kill me."

"If you don't think so keep stalling, or convince me I shouldn't pull this trigger and scatter your brains all over the inside of your car."

"You have to understand, I... Kelly was the only man who could pull this off. As Marco Toriago of course."

"I want to know how you found out who he is, and then I want to know about Grant and the stolen disk. Start talking."

"I can't tell you."

"Wrong answer." Merrick pulled the hammer back on his Beretta.

"Hell, Merrick!"

"My patience is running thin. I'm old, remember, and should have retired years ago. Maybe I've decided to take your advice. Maybe I'll just blow your head off and disappear."

"You're talking crazy."

"Crazy. Maybe I am."

"All right. The disk Grant stole is the SDECE's access code index. Locations, agent profiles, future mission agenda. You name it, it's there."

"A terrorist's Christmas list."

"Exactly."

"Who is behind this?"

Stillman shook his head.

Merrick pressed his gun against Stillman's temple. "Who?"

"We don't know."

"I used to be an assassin, remember? A damn good one. And before that, a mercenary for hire. Who?"

"Dammit, Merrick. We don't know who."

Stillman was sweating. Maybe he didn't have all the answers. Merrick eased the hammer back on the Beretta. "Let's talk about Grant. The agent you claimed died at Nescosto. But she didn't die, did she? You fabricated the entire story. A fabrication to me, the press, and your superiors."

"I had no choice, *mon ami.* If today you could get your hands on your wife's killer, what would you do? If it required you to blackmail someone, or falsify information, would you take the moral road, or cross the line?"

Merrick considered the question.

"I know what you'd do, Merrick. You'd cross that line in a second. We are alike in many ways, you and I. No price is too great to avenge a betrayal. Grant betrayed her country, and I'll do whatever it takes to save the SDECE."

"And yourself."

"I don't deny that I want to come out of this on top. It beats being buried."

"Tell me about Grant."

"What do you want to know? Besides her being a beautiful woman, she was a superb agent. I tell you, she was the best I've ever seen." Stillman filled Merrick in on how she'd disappeared in Munich. "Months later, she walked into my office and I almost fell off my chair. She said she had been held captive by a rebel group. She said she'd managed to escape. I guess I was so damn glad that she was back, I didn't see that there were subtle changes in her. Chanler noticed them, but I refused to examine why that might be. I made the excuse that she'd been busy trying to survive with criminals who were probably threatening to slit her throat every day. It was a good enough reason for her to be a little off her game."

"How off?"

"She didn't remember things. Little things. Chanler's kids' names, for one. Inside jokes. Agency procedure."

"Still, you put her back in the field."

"It was a busy time at the agency, and my superiors were climbing all over my ass. I had no choice. We needed her."

"Did she look like she'd spent time as a captive?"

"She was thinner. Grant's a brunette, but she colored her hair blond when she came to the agency six years ago. You know the statistics on blondes. Men love them. Anyway, her hair was grown out some. She looked tired. Like she'd been interrogated, possibly tortured. I did have some basic observation tests run. She came through them with no problem."

"How long was it before you put her back in the field?"

"Ten days."

"Ten days? How did you get your superiors to approve that?"

"I faked the records. Kept her off the field charts. No one knew but me and Chanler. Once she disappeared again, and I realized the disk was gone, I knew who had taken it."

"But you didn't tell your superiors."

"No. The disk was prepared with an acid overlay that once exposed to air, would vaporize the data in twenty-four hours. It was also encrypted. The SDECE is confident that the disk destroyed itself before it could be decoded."

"But you don't think so."

"The timing with Grant's disappearance makes me suspect. I never expressed my fears to the SDECE, however. Instead, I sent Chanler on vacation and filed a false report a month later fabricating a mission that I'd sent Chanler and Grant on. I padded the time she would have been in step-down being rehabilitated."

"Then you sent Chanler out into the field to hunt down Grant?"

"Yes. Chanler found her in Munich. Soon after, he lost her in Athens. I lost contact with him after that, and then one day I got an e-mail from him. All it said was that he was at Nescosto and that he'd found Grant. Two days later you blew Petrov's headquarters out of the water and took Chanler with it."

"But not Grant?"

"If she was there, she got out. Grant's alive, I feel it in my bones."

"That's when you decided to use Onyxx and Ash Kelly, which brings me back to my question. How did you learn Ash's true identity?"

Chapter 10

"You're sure he called her Jazmin Grant?"

"I sure as hell couldn't have made something like that up."

Ash continued to pace the floor in Sly's hotel suite. He had been playing the scenario over in his mind since they had left Ballvaro.

Sly asked, "Tell me again how you found her? From the moment you found Chanler with Grant. Hell, you're sure Nightingale is Jazmin Grant?"

"I was trying to get the crowd under control after the shots were fired when I saw her slip out the side door. I went after her, but by the time I got through the door she was headed for the courtyard. I followed. Heard the voices." Ash swore. "This is crazy. How could she be Grant? I thought I had this figured out. Boy, was I wrong."

Sly asked, "And you heard Chanler call her a traitor?"

"Yes, but she denied it."

"Of course she did. You said he was holding a gun on her at the time."

Ash swore. "I don't know. She got upset when he called her that. She said she was undercover."

Sly snorted. "At that point she would have said anything, don't you think?"

Ash felt sick. He should be seeing this in the same way Sly was, but he couldn't. Hell, maybe he just didn't want to. "She said Grant had to die, so she could go undercover. That's why she's got a new face and identity. Hell, I can relate to that." He turned and looked at Sly. "So can you."

"But we didn't do it to become a traitor," Sly reminded.

Ash stopped pacing. "Chanler's an arrogant sonofabitch. He's hasn't told us a thing."

"Would you? You shot him in the leg. He probably thinks you're working with her."

"I told him who we are."

"He doesn't know who he can trust. Maybe I should have a go at him."

"No. I've got a new angle. I'll try again."

"Take it easy on him. He's just acting like an agent whose partner stole a top secret disk, and handed it over to the enemy."

"I still think we're missing something." Ash began to pace again.

"Stillman says she's a traitor. Chanler believes it. She's got a new face and she's with Filip Petrov. It's pretty obvious that she's working for the enemy, Ash.

Sometimes things don't turn out like we want them to, but we still have to face the facts. When are you going to talk to her?"

"When I get back from seeing Chanler. If she's awake. That sedative really knocked her out."

"When you do, don't let her get to you."

Ash took offense. "I know how to do my job, Sly."

"Then do it. You might not like how this is going to play out, but you've got some pretty heavy evidence against her. It's obvious she's had some reconstruction done." Sly picked up a copy he'd made of the old Jazmin Grant. "Her nose and cheeks have been altered. Her lips are fuller. Even the mole is new. Hair and eye color could easily be explained away, but not the rest."

Ash turned away. He was still having trouble believing that Allegra was Jazmin Grant. There was no resemblance at all. But Sly was right, he couldn't dispute the facts. They were staring him in the face.

"I left another message on Merrick's phone to call me," Sly said.

"He still hasn't contacted you?"

"No."

"You worried?"

"It's not like him to ignore his messages. You going to call Stillman?"

"Not yet. I need to talk to Chanler first, then Alle— Jazmin Grant."

"And if Chanler can prove she's a traitor?"

Ash gave Sly a hard look. "If the pieces fit, then I'll have no choice but to believe the truth. But right now I don't know what that is, so I'm leaving the door open." He rubbed the back of his neck, then walked to the desk and started to round up the paperwork they had compiled on the mission—information that Sly had turned up, as well as the files that Stillman had given him in Paris. "I'll be in Naldo's suite talking to Chanler. I'll be back to talk to Jazmin Grant then. Keep an eye on her."

"You got it."

Ash left Sly's room and headed for Naldo's suite. He rapped on the door and Naldo promptly answered. He was wearing a serious face tonight. Things had started to heat up, and his easy-joking mood had been put on hold.

"How's Chanler?"

"He's pissed, and I had to gag him to keep him quiet. His leg wound is a minor inconvenience. I told him he shouldn't have tried to run."

Ash said, "If you need to step out and get some air, go ahead. Come back in an hour."

Once Naldo left, Ash entered the bedroom. Chanler was on the bed, eyes closed, his feet and hands manacled. Naldo had stuffed one of his socks in his mouth.

He opened his eyes when he heard the door close.

"Okay, Chanler, I'm going to take that sock out of your mouth and you and I are going to have another talk. If you decide not to cooperate, I'm going to shoot you again. Only this time, it's going to be a little higher, *comprendo*?" Ash removed the sock, then pulled a chair close to the bed and sat. "I'm not going to ask my questions twice, so listen good. As I said before, I work for the SDECE, we're comrades, and—"

"I don't believe you. If you want me to talk, call Stillman. He's the only person I'll talk to."

Ash swore. "I know the story. Grant took off with a disk and Stillman's been looking for her ever since. So my friend, if you're SDECE, why haven't you checked in with Stillman before now? He thinks you're dead. And another thing; if you had called him, then you would know that I was brought in to replace you."

Chanler considered what Ash said. "Give me something else to prove you're who you say you are."

"You have a wife and kids, and a dog. And Grant has been your partner from the beginning. Six years. Stillman always liked her better than you. He thought she was a superior agent."

"That bitch is a traitor!"

"Then help me prove it."

"Stillman sent me to hunt her down. I managed to locate her at Nescosto. I almost had her, then some asshole blew the place up. I managed to get out. Grant did too."

"So after Nescosto, you followed her here."

"Yes."

"Did you ambush the car at Ballvaro five days ago?"

"Yes."

"So you want her dead?"

"No, I want her to rot in prison, but I was beginning to think that was never going to happen. So I decided *dead* was better than nothing."

"Bad move."

"I admit it was a mistake. I've been in the field for months. I'd like to go home while my balls still work and before I'm bald."

"Do you know who she's working for?"

Chanler hesitated. "I need to speak to Stillman. If he okays it, then I'll tell you the rest."

Ash didn't want Stillman involved just yet. The bastard could have filled him in on half of this crap a week ago. He'd never trusted him, and he still didn't.

"The SDECE thinks you're dead, Chanler. So does your wife and kids."

The look on his face confirmed that Felton Chanler loved his wife and family. "They think I'm dead?"

"That's right. I sympathize with your situation, I really do. But that disk is somewhere in Budapest and I need to find it. So I want to know everything you know here and now, or your wife and kids will keep thinking you're dead." Ash smiled. "Dead and buried at Nescosto. So what's it going to be, Chanler? You going to tell me what I need to know, then make a phone call to you wife and ease her suffering, or are you going to stay dead?"

"I'm Allegra Nightingale."

That's right. Jazmin Grant is dead. You're Agent Nightingale now. An undercover agent."

"Who do I work for?"

"We fly no flag."

"You're a traitor. I followed the stench. Jazmin Grant, a traitor."

"Chanler!"

Allegra jerked awake and sat up.

No, she thought, it couldn't be true. She wasn't a traitor. She was an undercover agent. Chanler didn't know that, because no one was supposed to know. Not Stillman, not anyone.

But if that was true, then why did she feel so sick inside? Like something was terribly wrong, and that it was all her fault?

She clutched her head, as a memory stole her breath. It was as if someone had pressed the reverse button, then hit fast forward. It fractured her thinking, and she was suddenly remembering bits and pieces.

Munich.

Cyrus.

Athens.

She heard the door open, and she expected to see Toriago walk in. He'd rescued her at Ballvaro in the courtyard.

She would be in debt to him again, but right now she didn't care about that. She just needed to remember.

To her surprise it was a stranger who walked into the room. He was tall and built like a machine. Handsome in a dangerous way that reminded her of Toriago.

"You're awake. Good."

"I must have been given something. What was it?"

"A sedative. You were pretty hysterical."

She had good reason, she thought. Chanler had accused her of treason. "Who are you?"

"My name's Sly McEwen. Who are you?"

"I'm Allegra Nightingale."

He frowned. "She doesn't really exist. We know that. I was talking about your real name."

He knew who she was. "Where's Toriago?"

"Out right now."

"I need to make a phone call."

"Sorry, that's going to have to wait, Miss Grant."

"I really need to make a phone call."

"And who would you call?"

"I…can't tell you that. Where's Chanler?"

"He's busy right now."

"Busy or dead?"

"He's alive. His leg wound is minor. Where's the disk?"

"What disk?"

"The one you stole from the SDECE."

She slumped back against the headboard. What had she done? God, she wished she could remember. Was it true? Was she a traitor?

"Tell me what your mission is, then maybe we'll let you make that phone call."

"We?"

He leaned into the door jamb and crossed his arms over his broad chest. He was very cool, as if he was used to interrogating the enemy.

The enemy? Was she the enemy?

"The mission? You were about to tell me what you're doing in Budapest. Does it involve the disk?"

She had no idea what she was doing in Budapest, and an agent always knew what her mission was. But she didn't, and that fact made her wonder if Chanler was right. *Had* she been used in some way?

"It would be better if you cooperated with us. Ash isn't too happy with you right now. When he's not happy, it's hard to tell what he might do."

"Who's Ash?"

"He's…the tough guy in this outfit."

"And you're the good guy, Mr. McEwen?"

"I guess."

"Not a very original game."

He waited, but she wasn't going to tell him anything. She had to make a phone call. But who would she call? If Cyrus had tricked her, then she couldn't call him.

And if Stillman believed she was a traitor, he would never buy her story that she had no idea what was going on.

"Suit yourself." He started out the door, then turned back. "I'll let Ash know you're awake."

"I want to see Toriago."

"Is she awake?" Ash asked.

"She's in the bathroom."

Ash had just stepped back into Sly's suite after interrogating Chanler. The man had spilled his guts on the pretense he was going to get to call his wife.

Ash had promised him he could make the call, but it hadn't worked out that way. Right now it was better if Stillman continued to believe that Chanler was still dead. A call to his wife would have ended all that.

Chanler wasn't happy right now—he'd called Ash every name in the book, and then some.

He'd gotten so loud that he was again wearing Naldo's sock.

"Get anything out of him?"

"He talked this time."

"And do you believe him?"

Ash didn't want to, but it looked like Jazmin Grant had sold out the SDECE. At least, that was Chanler's story, and he had a good case against her.

"He claims Stillman ignored his warning about Grant after she disappeared the first time. He says after she took off the second time, Stillman sent him after her. He was at Nescosto when we took it down."

"Looking for Grant?"

"He claims she was there. It holds up if Allegra

Nightingale is in fact Jazmin Grant. We know she was with Filip, and he came to Budapest straight from Nescosto."

Sly nodded. "And when Nescosto fell and Stillman thought Chanler was dead, he went to Onyxx and pulled you in. Everything fits."

"Does it?"

Sly sighed. "Come on, Ash. It's all right in front of you. Why don't you want to believe it?"

Ash turned his back on Sly. "Maybe because I know what will happen to her when I take her back."

"It was her choice. By the way, I talked to her. From what she's not saying, I think she's guilty as hell. She wants to make a phone call. I'll give one guess who that will be to."

"I said I wanted to be the first one to talk to her."

"As Ash Kelly?"

"What does that mean?"

"She wants to talk to Toriago. Is there something more between you two than you're letting on? We could take her back to Washington if you want to step back. There are ways to make her talk."

Ash had sat in on interrogation sessions at Onyxx. They were no picnic.

"I'll handle it." He started down the hall.

"You think you're up to it?"

He turned around. "What?"

"It's hard to see things clearly when you're not thinking entirely with your head."

"Are you questioning my loyalty?"

"Should I be?"

Maybe Sly was right to ask him that, but he wasn't

going to hang her until he knew she deserved the noose. "I'll get the truth out of her," Ash said. "If she's guilty, then I'll do what has to be done."

He walked down hall and opened the bathroom door without giving her any warning. The sudden intrusion surprised her, but it also surprised Ash.

She had stripped off the party gown and she was naked. Naked and covered in bruises.

"What the hell happened?"

She grabbed the towel to shield herself. "Toriago? God, I'm glad to see you. I need your help."

"What kind of help, Jaz?"

"Jaz? Why would you call me that?"

"Because I know who you are. You're Jazmin Grant and you've been missing from the SDECE for months. Now I need some answers. The first one is who beat you up?"

She shook her head and backed up.

"Come on, Jaz, I'm here to help."

She clutched the towel closer to her naked body. "The bruises are a little present from Filip. He wasn't happy with me after you told him I used your phone and that we slept together."

"I didn't tell him that. I didn't tell him anything."

"Then how did he know?"

"I don't know."

Ash took the robe off the hook behind the door. "Here. Put this on."

He helped her slip it on, and when she dropped the towel, he carefully tied the belt around her waist.

"Who's the guy who's been guarding me?"

"A friend of mine." Ash waited, hoped she would

start talking. When she didn't say any more, he said, "Chanler says you're a traitor. Are you?"

"No. Now I have a question for you. Who are you, Toriago, and why are you so interested in me?"

"Remember when I told you my offer had no time limit? Talk to me, and maybe I can keep you alive long enough to figure this mess out."

"Ash." Sly rapped on the door. "It's Merrick on the phone. He wants to talk to you."

"You're Ash?"

If he had started to break a little ground, it had suddenly been shot to hell. The look on her face told him that they were going to have to start over.

So they would start over. When two people met for the first time there was usually an introduction.

He said, "Like you, I have two names. Right now you're talking to Ash Kelly. I could be your worst nightmare, or your saving grace. It's up to you, Jazmin Grant. Think on that while I'm gone."

Ash disconnected the phone and set the cell on the desk, then he hit a button on Sly's computer and waited a few seconds.

"We need to identify this guy," he said as soon as the picture popped up. "The one you pulled from Chanler's file."

"Why didn't you tell Merrick you have her?"

Ash turned. "We're not going to get along too well, Sly, if you keep questioning every move I make. Once I have the whole story, I'll show my hand. Handing Grant over now won't get us the disk. She must know where it is."

"Like I said, there are ways to make her talk." Sly looked over his shoulder at the computer screen. "It's going to be damn hard to identify him."

"Maybe she can do it for us."

"No time like the present."

Ash saw Sly glance past him. He turned around, and there standing in the hall was Jazmin Grant.

He still couldn't believe that Allegra Nightingale and Jazmin Grant were one and the same. But maybe she was having trouble buying his story, too.

She was clutching the front of her robe, and it reminded him of the damage that Petrov had done when he'd worked her over. Her stomach and ribs were a mass of black and purple bruises, and although she hid it well, she had to be in a lot of pain.

The crazy thing was, when he looked at her, he didn't see a traitor. It didn't matter who he was looking at. Neither identity fit the MO of a traitor. But then he'd been wrong about so many things, maybe he was wrong about this, too. What he wasn't wrong about was those bruises. If she was a player on Petrov's team, why the hell had he beaten her up? That didn't make sense.

But it wasn't enough to vindicate her. In fact, the proof was piling up against her, and if she didn't start talking soon he would have no choice but to turn her over to Merrick and Stillman.

Hell, Merrick and Stillman working together? That was about as unbelievable as the rest of this mess.

Ash motioned her into the room. "I've got something here for you to take a look at."

She walked slowly toward him. "What is it?"

"Do you remember when this picture was taken?"

She stopped next to him and stared down at the computer screen, then she looked from Sly to Ash. "That was while I was in Munich."

"Doing what?"

"I don't remember exactly. A mission, I suppose."

"Recognize the guy walking away from you?" Ash asked.

She looked at the photo. "His name is Cyrus. I don't think he ever told me his last name."

Ash glanced at Sly. "Run the name."

When Ash looked back at her, he saw she was again staring at the picture. Only this time, her hand was touching her face, examining her nose and cheeks, then following the shape of her lips.

Ash studied her expression. It was as if she was seeing a misplaced relative or friend that she had almost forgotten existed.

Finally, she said, "I'm tired. I'll be in the bedroom."

When she had left the room, Sly exploded. "Why didn't you press her for more answers?"

"Did you see the way she looked at herself in that picture? Something's not right. She's processing this like she's not sure what's going on. I think she's as confused as we are."

"So what now?"

"Can you relieve Naldo for a few hours? I've got an errand I'd like him to run for me and I don't want to leave Chanler unguarded."

"I can do that. What are you planning?"

"I need to gain her trust."

"That's not going to happen, Ash. You've got to

come up with something else here. Because that's going to fly about as well as a bird with busted wings."

"Break down the computer and work on finding out who Cyrus is while you're keeping an eye on Chanler. Oh, and call Merrick back and tell him that we've identified the guy in the picture. See if Chanler can verify his identity, and put a last name on him."

Chapter 11

Two hours later, his plan in motion, Ash slipped into the bedroom. "I know you're not sleeping, so sit up and listen."

She opened her eyes and sat up. "Time to torture me, Mr. Kelly?"

"Get dressed."

"All I have to wear is that dress." She motioned to the gold ball-buster she'd worn to the party at Ballvaro.

"It works for me. Put it on."

She hesitated.

"I've seen you naked, bruises and all. Get dressed."

"Why?"

"We're getting out of here."

"Where are we going?"

"You'll find out soon enough. Get dressed, unless you want to wear that robe out of here."

She didn't argue further. She climbed off the bed, slipped out of the robe, and wearing nothing but a gold thong, picked up the dress and wiggled into it.

"I picked up your shoes where you left them at Ballvaro." He motioned to them on the floor next to the desk.

It was close to midnight, and Sly was still babysitting Chanler—the ideal place for him to be while Ash disappeared with Jaz. He didn't like leaving his friend in the dark, but right now he didn't think Sly was going to agree to anything but handing Jaz over to Stillman, or pulling her fingernails out by the roots until she gave up the location of the disk.

He ushered her through the door, then draped his leather jacket over her shoulders. Naldo was in the living room, wearing a look of concern on his face.

He hadn't been crazy about Ash's idea from the moment he'd relayed it to his cousin, but unlike Sly, Naldo was used to playing by no rules. And when your back was up against the wall, sometimes that was the only way to play out your hand.

"You sure you want to do it this way, *primo*? Maybe I should come with you."

"No. Hang around here for another hour, then go back to your room. If Sly's still working on that name, leave him be. The longer he stays away from here the better. I don't need him taking chase. I'll be in touch."

Ash walked to the door and opened it, then said to Naldo, "You know what to do. Be there on time."

"Be where?" The question came from Jaz.

Ash didn't answer her. Instead he handcuffed her wrist to his. "I read your profile. Never trust a woman who can outrun you and sprint a three-minute mile."

The handcuffs had ruined Jaz's plan to escape, and once they were in the limo, he'd cuffed her to the door, and added a blindfold.

Jaz tried to concentrate on the noises, but once they left the city, she had no idea what direction they were going.

"Don't you think this is a little extreme?" she said from the backseat. She knew the window between the seats was down, and that he had no trouble hearing her.

"Like I said, I read your profile. I imagine so did your new boss."

"He said that was why I was chosen."

"Chosen?"

"Yes. For the undercover work. Where are we going?"

"To a place where we can be alone, and you can pull it together."

"Pull what together?"

"Right now you're a traitor in the eyes of the intelligence world. If you still maintain that you're innocent of that accusation, I suggest you pull it together and start convincing me that you're the victim in a plot of subterfuge."

"Is that what you think I am?"

"You tell me."

"You lost your accent."

"It comes and goes depending on who I am. I'm sure

you can relate to that. It seems on this mission, no one is who they seem to be."

"And exactly who are you? Who do you work for?" Jaz asked.

"I'm the man who hasn't convicted you yet. This Cyrus, do you know where I can find him?"

Jaz couldn't answer that, not if she even wanted to. Ash Kelly might seem to be on her side, but she couldn't trust him. How could she trust him after he'd handcuffed and blindfolded her?

"I'm risking my ass here, honey, on a hunch. It would be nice if you'd appreciate my efforts."

"I never asked you to risk your ass. By the way, you never said who you work for."

"The SDECE."

"I don't believe you."

They had been driving a long time. It must have been close to an hour. Suddenly, the car slowed down, and then it stopped altogether.

Jaz heard a door open and when a crisp gust of cold air entered the backseat, she knew he'd gotten out of the limo. He was gone for several minutes, and when he came back he opened the back door and unlocked the handcuff from around the door handle.

Free, she pulled the blindfold off and looked around. In the distance she saw a small cabin surrounded by trees.

"Slide out. Careful. There's snow on the ground."

He wasn't rough or hostile when he took hold of her arm. In fact, he was slow and careful as he helped her out of the backseat of the limo. He even put his hand on the top of her head to guide her out, and made sure his jacket remained around her shoulders.

"What do you think?" he said. "Like it?"

"What's there to like? I'm stuck with you in the middle of nowhere."

"Exactly. It's perfect. Come on."

He was leading her by the handcuff, and she swore when she nearly toppled on the ground after her shoe slipped.

"Damn shoes."

"But they look great."

"And keep me from running."

"You read my mind."

"I don't believe that you're SDECE. Filip recognized the name Toriago. And Salavich did, too."

"We all have a past."

"What does that mean?"

"It means, I was Marco Toriago a few years ago, and I wasn't very nice."

"Well, from where I'm standing nothing, has changed. Who do you think Cyrus is?"

"I think he's an international criminal with a lot of power and money. He had to have both to pull this off."

Jaz stopped. "He can't be. You're wrong."

"Why?"

"Cyrus can't be a criminal. He's the head of an underground intelligence operation. He has to be."

"I don't think so."

"He has to be! Don't you understand? If he's who you say he is, then I'm…"

"Now you're getting it. I thought a drive and some time away would clear the cobwebs upstairs."

Not all of them, Jaz thought, but she was starting to see a few things more clearly. And if Ash Kelly was right, and he was here because he believed her, then he was the only one she could trust.

The problem was, she didn't do trust. Then why did she want to trust him so badly?

The Petnehazy was a complex of private bungalows for people who wanted to escape and enjoy being pampered, or at least that's how the ad had read.

Ash had decided that if he could get Jaz alone maybe she would open up to him. Sly meant well, but he was an in-your-face kind of guy, and in this case what Jazmin Grant needed was a gentler approach.

More than ever Ash was convinced that Jaz had been the pawn in some bizarre plot. A criminal plot designed by a man named Cyrus.

He had only a few hours to figure it all out. He damn well hoped that he wasn't thinking with another part of his body instead of his head, as Sly had suggested.

It was true he had feelings for Jazmin Grant. No, he had feelings for Allegra Nightingale. If Jazmin Grant had been used as a pawn, then they were one and the same.

To prove that she wasn't a traitor, she was going to have to work with him, not against him.

He only hoped that there was time enough for her to see that.

He pulled a key from his pocket and opened the bungalow he'd had Naldo rent. He flipped on the light and then pulled her inside and closed the door.

"This is home until tomorrow, Jaz. Just you and me."

She looked around, then pulled his jacket from her shoulders. "Where is this place?"

"If I wanted you to know that, I wouldn't have blind-folded you."

She turned. "Your real name is…"

"My birth name is Marco Toriago. Today I'm Ash Kelly, SDECE."

"What's in a name, right?"

"We both have a couple, it's true. But who we are underneath is what counts. And that's what we're here to find out. There's not much time, and I know you don't *do* trust. You do cause and effect. So here is the scenario. You stole a disk from the SDECE *causing* them to become vulnerable to an international criminal. The *effect* of that act will collapse the SDECE, and will ultimately get you killed in the end if you did it knowing that the choice you made was seditious. We're here to prove that you were either a willing participant, or that you were blinded by one man's treachery. Again, I'll tell you that I want to believe that an agent with a spotless record wouldn't succumb to treason. Am I wrong?"

"No. You're not wrong. I'm no traitor."

"Good."

"That's it? You believe me just like that?"

"I want to believe you, so let's go with that for now."

He saw her press her hand into her side, and it reminded him that she was still battling the effects of Filip's beating.

"Here, let's get you out of that dress and into the whirlpool."

She looked at him as if he was joking.

"I did the research. I'm told the mineral spas here do wonders for an aching body. Maybe once you start feeling more like yourself, you'll start thinking more like Jaz Grant."

Ash stepped forward and unzipped the back of her dress. "I'm sure you can take it from there. I'll start a fire and get the jets going in the whirlpool. Would you like some wine, or a martini? Gin, right?"

"He did what!"

Merrick was livid.

"I should have expected it," Sly said over the phone. "He wasn't acting like himself. I should have suspected something when he didn't tell you we had Jazmin Grant."

Merrick looked over his shoulder at Stillman, who was boring a hole in his back. He walked away and lowered his voice. "He has Grant?"

"Yes. And we have Chanler."

"He's alive, too."

"Yes."

This time Merrick turned to Stillman and pointed. "You've got more explaining to do."

To Sly, he said, "So what's the plan?"

"Plan? Ah, I haven't got one yet. I was hoping I'd hear from Ash soon."

"You think that's going to happen?"

"I'm hopeful."

"Now we're working on hope. I'll be sure to put that in my report. I think it'll be a first."

"At the moment, that's the best I've got."

"Well, your best sucks."

"This is so screwed up it's going to take a psychic to figure it out. Something else you should know. She identified the guy in the picture."

"Who is it?"

"She called him Cyrus."

Merrick's stomach did a complete flip, and he swore his heart stopped for several seconds. "You're sure she said Cyrus?"

"I'm sure. Chanler can't identify him, so we have to go on her word."

"A traitor's word?"

"Ash thinks she'd been sucked in somehow. I think that's why he took off with her. He's not convinced this is just a case of an agent gone bad. You still there?"

Merrick's world was still spinning after hearing the name. It couldn't be *his* Cyrus. That was impossible.

"Merrick, are you there?"

"I'm here."

"The name Cyrus…it sounds familiar. Wasn't that the name of one of your old teammates years ago?"

"Yes. Someone else who is supposed to be dead."

"Do you think she's right?"

"Do I think Cyrus Krizova is alive? Yesterday I would have said no. Today I'm not sure of anything. When Ash makes contact with you tell him to call me."

Merrick hung up the phone and turned to Stillman. "Chanler's alive. How long have you known that?"

"He's alive?"

"Cut the crap."

"I'm as surprised by the news as you are. Where is he?"

"In Budapest with one of my men."

"Then we go to Budapest."

"No, not yet. We wait for—" Merrick's phone went off again. Thinking it might be Ash, he answered quickly. "Merrick here." He paused.

"What? When? How many dead?"

Merrick's gut did another flip as he was relayed the information.

"They say it was a gas leak. That's bull. I'll be on the next flight."

When he disconnected this time he sat down.

"What's going on, Merrick?"

"My apartment building in Washington. Someone blew it up tonight."

"I thought I heard 'gas leak'?"

"It was no gas leak."

The minute he said the words, he was punching in another set of numbers on his phone. Sarah. Oh, God. She would have gone to feed the cat after work.

Wanting to trust someone and being able to were two different things. But if Ash Kelly was right? Then she'd been a pawn in Cyrus's plot to destroy the SDECE.

All the old loyalties were rushing back now. All Jaz's memories of her life at the SDECE. How had she been so willing to forget them all, or had that been part of his plan?

You were chosen. The best of the best. It's an honor, Nightingale.

Her greatest fear was not remembering what he had stolen from her. Everything was fragmented. And what if that was part of the beauty of it all, that she would never be able to fit the pieces together?

She heard the whirlpool start up and turned to see Ash Kelly squatting beside the sunken tub.

He looked up. "I've seen you naked, so you don't have to be shy with me."

"You have not seen me naked."

He grinned. "It's a little late to be modest, don't you think?"

"That's right, you're not into skinny women."

"Who told you that?"

"You didn't like what you saw the last time, and nothing's changed."

He stood, and pulled off his sweater. He was all muscle, and she remembered what it felt like to touch him. It was crazy how he had slipped into her life so easily. She was no longer afraid to trust him.

Of all people, why would she trust a man who had two different names and carried explosives around like Life Savers?

Of all people, why would *he* trust a woman with two different names, and two faces?

"One thing we should clear up," he said. "I liked what I saw the other night, make no mistake about that. But I'm a selfish guy. When I make love to a woman, I want her on the same page. I want her wanting what I want. You were in my room to make a phone call. If you hadn't been caught, you wouldn't have played the seduction card. You were very good at it, by the way."

"Obviously not good enough. You left with a hard-on and I went to bed…" She stopped herself from giving away the disappointment she'd felt when he'd walked out that night.

"Finish it." He came toward her. "You went to bed…"

"Alone," she finished.

He walked around her and stopped behind her. His hands settled on her shoulders and then he slid the straps of gold down her arms, his fingers moving slowly, tugging the straps past her elbows.

"A seduction of your own, Ash Kelly?"

"That depends on what you want. If Toriago was here, he would take you in a second. Against the wall. On the floor. Standing right here. Ash Kelly...well, he's..."

She turned around, her hands moving upward to rescue the bodice of her dress from falling away. "He's what? Finish it," she said, using his words.

"The man I was eight years ago retired. Those were wild days, and I was free to do and be whoever I wanted to be. Free until prison. That was a wake-up call. Since then, Ash Kelly has reformed a bit. He's no slouch, and he doesn't back down to anyone. And when he kills someone, it's for a better reason than drugs or money. Would you like that glass of wine now? Or have you decided on the gin martini?"

"Wine."

"Red or white?"

"White." She watched him walk away. She'd studied him for days, but she realized tonight was the first time she was really seeing him for who he was. Partly because the game was over, she imagined, but as taken as she had been with Toriago, she suddenly found herself anxious to get to know Ash Kelly.

While his back was turned, she slipped out of the dress and let it fall to the floor. Stepping out of it, she slid the thong past her thighs, then walked down the steps into the whirlpool of warm, steamy water, removing the bracelet on her wrist, and setting it on the ledge, she relaxed back against the tiles and closed her eyes.

The water felt heavenly and her body began to relax. He was right, she needed this, needed this time to think back to those months with Cyrus.

She had to put the pieces together and remember how she could have been led astray by an imposter. A very good, very rich imposter—he'd had the means to convince her that everything he said was true. But how had he done that?

And where had he taken her? It reminded her of an old monastery. Somewhere not far from Athens, Greece. He'd told her it was one of many underground intelligence bases. How could she have been so gullible?"

Think.

Remember.

"Here."

She opened her eyes and saw Ash crouching down with his hand extended.

"White wine."

"Thank you." She took the glass and said, "Are you going to join me?"

"I'll pass on the drink, but the water looks inviting, and the company."

"I'm not afraid to believe you anymore."

"That's a good start."

He stepped out of his pants, leaving his tight-legged black briefs on. They accented his muscular thighs and…the rest of his perfection.

He came into the water, sat down across from her, and relaxed against the wall.

Ash Kelly was gentler than Toriago. He'd said prison had been a wake-up call. That he no longer killed without reason. She wondered if he had to have a better reason for making love than just wanting to, because right now, that was all she wanted.

"So, Jaz, come up with any memories you'd like to share? Maybe you should start with the first time you disappeared from the SDECE."

"I was in Munich when Cyrus first approached me. He told me that I had been cleared to go with him."

"And so you went?"

"Yes."

"Where?"

"To Athens."

"Greece?"

"Yes. But from there I don't know where he took me. He explained that I would be transported to the base in a cabin on a yacht."

"And you agreed?"

"Yes."

"And that's where Jaz Grant died and Allegra Nightingale was born?"

"I know it sounds unreal. But it's true." Jaz looked away from him. "I can't believe I never second-guessed his motives."

"He's very good. Don't blame yourself."

She looked at him. "Then who do I blame?"

"Bad luck. The weather. Whatever you want."

"Why are you being so nice to me? Your friend thinks I'm a traitor. Why don't you?"

"A few things don't add up."

"Just a few, and you're willing to gamble on those odds?"

He shrugged. "What can I say, I'm a sucker for mystery women? I think it's interesting that you can remember your childhood, but more current events are blurry."

"It's true, I remember my life in France with my mother. Bonnie has been with me."

"Bonnie's your mother?"

"Yes. Who I am is because of her. She taught me how to survive. Not to expect too much, and to take what I needed. There's a balance, you know."

"Yes, I learned that a little late. But I've got it now. So you were brought to this facility twice?"

"Yes. But I don't remember much about the second time."

"Drugged, you think."

"Maybe." Jaz took a sip of her wine, then set the glass on the ledge. She brought her hands to her face and then sent them up through her hair. She wished she could remember more to help him help her. "This isn't going to work. I don't remember enough. I know now that was his plan. He must have wiped out pieces of my memory with drugs or something else."

"We're going to get him. I promise you that."

His voice had turned hard-edged. He meant what he said.

"I just don't know why he picked me."

"I do. He needed someone from the SDECE, and so he went to the top. Stillman says you're the best, and I have to agree. I've seen your stats."

"You know it's very strange that I like you. I don't like many men."

His face softened. "I'm a lucky guy, then."

"I don't know about that. I'm worried that I won't be able to help you stop whatever is about to happen."

"What's going to happen is that Filip is about to turn the city upside-down to find you."

"And when he does?"

"Who says he'll find you?"

"But if he does?"

"You let me worry about Filip."

"What if I don't remember what happened to the disk before we run out of time?"

When he didn't answer, her heart sank.

"That bad." She looked away from him, again. "I can't live never remembering, and never knowing the extent of what I've done. If you know, why don't you just tell me? Maybe it will open my eyes and jolt my memory."

"I know you stole a disk, and that you're no traitor. I just need to recover the data on that disk and…"

"And what?"

"Convince Stillman that you're not a traitor. Now enough talk. Let the water relax you, and try to forget about it for a while." He stood and walked toward her, sat down beside her. "We'll sort it out later."

"If you were in my shoes, could you live with it?"

"Live with what?"

"Everyone thinking you're a traitor."

"I don't know."

"Well, I know. I can't."

She stood up suddenly, forgetting she was naked. The minute the cool air touched her skin she realized her mistake. He had to be staring at her bare ass right now. She didn't move, didn't say anything.

After several seconds, he said, "Turn around."

Slowly, she turned. "We're not going to be able to fix this, are we?"

"Not right now. Come back and sit down." He reached out and tugged her down onto the bench. "How are your ribs feeling?"

"Much better."

"And the bruises on your stomach?"

She looked into his eyes. They were so easy to read just now. "Why do you care?"

"Maybe I like you, too."

She smiled. "Maybe?"

"Okay, I like you. I guess the truth is I did the first day I saw you. But you already know that. There's been something going on between us since you dove into my car head first. But don't worry, I didn't bring you here for selfish reasons. This is about you and getting you to feel better, not me."

"What would make you feel better?"

He let out a long sigh. "I'm fine."

"But you could be better, right?"

He reached out and traced her mouth with a wet finger, leaving water drops behind. "How did he explain the reason for giving you a new face?"

"When you're under deep cover, you can't have a past unless it's useful. Mine wasn't."

"The changes are subtle, but they certainly altered your looks."

"It took a while to believe it was me staring back in the mirror."

He seemed to be dissecting her face. Finally, he said, "You were okay with the face change?"

"Cyrus said no sacrifice was too great. That when you're chosen, sacrifices must be made. I admit I was nervous, but I…"

"You what?"

"I'm a natural brunette. For the SDECE, I bleached it blond as part of my look. My role as an agent was internal sabotage. The recovery operations involved a higher rate of men than women. As you know most people think blondes are a bit more daring and exciting. I was curvy back then, and I admit the look was … Well, I would have been able to support myself quite well as a stripper."

She saw him grin, then look down.

"What is it? Did I say something funny?"

"It's what I thought when I saw your picture." He looked up. "No disrespect."

"None taken. When my mother was alive she used to entertain men for money. The neighbors called her a whore, but she wasn't. She didn't have much education, but she was beautiful. I loved Bonnie, and with every year that passes I respect her sacrifices more and more. She was a good mother, and she never lied to me. She knew what was important, when and why to take a risk, and how far to go without losing yourself. The irony in that is, I lost control of that choice when Cyrus interrupted my life months ago.

"You know I joined the SDECE because I thought I could make a difference. I know that sounds a bit naive, but I knew I could do it. It wasn't all glamorous and normal, and maybe that was the appeal. I've always enjoyed using my mind, and being athletic. Not that I haven't used my body, too. I'll admit it was a tool I relied on for certain missions. The old Jazmin Grant was a bold bitch, a blend of brains and curves, and she never gave up."

"And Allegra Nightingale?"

"She's twenty pounds thinner and a bit more reserved, but no less determined. I might not look the same, but there are a few of the old parts still hanging around. Sometimes when I look in the mirror I expect to see *her* looking back at me. I've had a nose job, cheek implants and more collagen injected in my lips than a French model."

"And your eyes?"

"Green contacts."

"You weren't afraid?"

"Cyrus sold me on his plan. What more can I say? He kept saying I was chosen. That being recruited into a deep cover agency was an honor. I bought it, as well as the need for reconstructive surgery."

His hand touched her cheek. "I like how honest you are."

"Then you really do believe me?"

"Yes."

"And where does that leave us exactly, Ash Kelly?"

"I don't know yet. At the moment, I'm doing the best I can to stay focused on the job, but…"

"And how is that working for you so far?"

His hand slid around the back of her neck, and he leaned in and kissed her gently. "It's not working too well. It's getting harder by the second."

"Are we talking situation or anatomy now?"

He grinned. "Cute."

She leaned her head against the rim of the tub and closed her eyes. She didn't speak again, and neither did he. After a long minute, she opened one eye and found that he'd closed his eyes, too, and that his breathing was slow and deep.

She sat up and pushed herself away from the wall. Placing her hands on the tiled rim on either side of his head, she straddled him.

She had just begun to ease herself down onto his lap when he opened his eyes. "I was wondering what you were going to do to relieve the pain you're in."

"Did I say I was in pain?"

"Either that's what I'm feeling, or we've been joined by a sea serpent."

"The woman makes jokes while I'm suffering."

"You said I had a sense of humor."

"I did, didn't I?" He sobered. "Here's the deal. I didn't bring you here to seduce you. You took a helluva beating from Petrov and you could use a night to rest and—"

"And remember the past few months."

"That too."

Jaz started to get off him. "All you had to say was that you weren't interested. You didn't need to list your reasons."

His hands settled on her hips and kept her welded to his lap. "I'm interested. You can feel that I am. I just don't want this to be about me."

"Another visit from the Boy Scout. Are you always this unselfish?"

"I'm not unselfish. I just don't want you looking back on this with any regrets."

She leaned in and kissed him. "If you want me, then we're on common ground. Does that help?"

She must have said the right words because suddenly his hands were moving up her back, urging her closer. Her breasts touched his chest, and the warm water and steam moved around them. And for now it was only the two of them in the whirlpool, no past and no Cyrus.

When he kissed her long and deep, she knew what had started days ago had begun again. Only this time the outcome would be very different, and she answered his kiss with one of her own—a kiss that sent her on a new journey.

One Bonnie would have warned her was the death of all women who believed there was such a thing as common ground between a man and a woman.

Chapter 12

When the Chameleon heard Filip Petrov's voice on the phone, he knew something was wrong.

"What is it? What's gone wrong, Filip?"

"There was a shooting at Ballvaro tonight. Allegra's disappeared."

"Disappeared?"

The Chameleon listened to Filip while he relayed what had happened. All the while his blood pressure began to rise as he puffed on his Cuban cigar.

Nightingale missing? "Did she run, or was she taken?"

"I don't know."

"You don't know?" The Chameleon puffed harder, the blue smoke settling around him like a dark omen. "You disappoint me, Filip. I would expect a man in your vulnerable position to be concerned with proving his worth. You were scheduled to deliver the data tomorrow for decoding, and now—"

"I still can. I thought you had a tracker on her."

"Yes, that's true. But what if she's already out of the country—"

"I don't think so."

"From now on, I'll do the thinking, Filip. So you will wait to hear from me, and you had better hope that she's close by. Without Nightingale all is lost, and if that is the case, so are you."

"Then I'll wait for your call."

"Yes, you will. I'll call back with her location within the hour. You see, Filip, unlike you, I never make a mistake. I've learned over the years to double my odds. You should try it some time."

When the Chameleon hung up he headed into the bowels of *Minare* to locate Barinski. When he reached the corridor, he heard laughter.

He followed the laughter, and when he opened the door into the regeneration room he found Melita sitting on a table with her legs crossed eating an apple. Barinski was seated three feet away. They both looked up in surprise on hearing the door open, and when the good doctor saw who had interrupted his late-night party, he jerked to his feet, tipping over the chair.

"This is cozy," the Chameleon said.

Melita continued to munch on her apple, while Barinski fumbled for his glasses, forgetting for a moment that they were riding his forehead.

Jerking them into place, he said, "We were just talking, and—"

"Melita, go to your room."

She uncrossed her legs and slid off the table. "I didn't know I had a curfew."

"Go now, before I decide to give you one."

She walked past him, then turned. "Don't let your imagination run wild, Father. Nigel was just telling me some stories about his years in Nuremberg. I haven't forgotten what you're capable of, so don't do something irreversible. Like hang him from the rafters and flog him to death."

The suggestion sent Barinski's hand to his neck, his pale skin turning blue with the suggestion—death by suffocation.

She gave Nigel a playful wink. "I enjoyed the stories, Nigel. Thank you. If you're still alive in the morning, I'll see you in the laboratory."

When she left, the Chameleon said, "Nightingale is missing and you need to locate her for me."

"That shouldn't be difficult. I've planned for any obstacle that should arise."

Somehow that wasn't very reassuring, the Chameleon thought. He'd had nothing but setbacks since some damn fool had blown up Nescosto. He was just damn lucky that Nightingale had survived.

The Chameleon followed Barinski out the door and into the soundproof cubicle. There, Dr. Frankenstein turned on the high-frequency tracking monitor. It took only a matter of minutes for the transmitter to lock on its target and pinpoint her location.

The good news was, Nightingale was still in Budapest. The bad news was, her progesterone levels were over the roof.

"It seems you didn't plan for every obstacle, Barinski. Whoever she's with is getting the ride of his life."

She stripped off his shorts, and then she was back, straddling him and turning him inside out with her warm body.

"Maybe we should slow down."

It wasn't something Marco Toriago would have said. But then again, Toriago had never had a problem finishing what he'd started.

Ash was turned on, stone hard and hungry, but the question still remained, could he deliver the goods and bring it home?

"It's been a while for me," she whispered against his lips, then raised up, slid forward, and slowly swallowed him up as she settled in his lap again. "If I'm rushing you, I'm sorry."

It's been a while.

More common ground.

"Have you ever watched a thunderstorm?" she asked.

"I suppose I have."

She was smiling down at him. "Most of the thunderstorms I've watched start out with a lightning show. You know, fast and quick. Explosive."

"Explosive, yeah. I can relate to collateral damage."

She sat up, then slowly fed him back inside her.

"And how does a thunderstorm relate to us?" he asked.

"Maybe if we're lucky lightning will strike twice. You know, since I'm in such a rush this time."

Hell, he was praying that he could pull off one explosion. And she was already planning for the next rain cloud.

"Are you going to be all right? I mean those bruises are—"

"Waterlogged, and I feel fine. Better than fine. I'm not as fragile as I look. And I'm with the Boy Scout, remember? I think I'm in good hands."

Toriago was the one with good hands. They might have the same tools, but they used them differently. Hell, he hadn't used them at all in a year.

Ash slid his hands over her ass and began to move, setting the rhythm in long, swift motions that sent her moaning and arching her hips.

The pace established, she set the tone, kissing him and touching him, and setting him on fire—lighting the fuse for the explosion that would surely take his head off one way or the other.

Her lips were parted, her eyes focused on him. Her hands were on his shoulders, her long legs hugging him so tight.

God, she was beautiful, and he had never wanted any woman as much as he wanted her right now.

Her warm breasts were teasing his chest as they rose in and out of the water with her rapid hip action. He closed his eyes a moment, moaned with the pleasure she was giving him. He felt her body begin to spasm and it sucked him deeper inside her.

The pressure built, dragging him down that familiar road. He let go at that moment, and a guttural groan followed him into the frenzy of two bodies engaged in the dance of life. He was right about the rush going to his head.

He rode it out, that moment when life and death has no meaning, just the euphoria of feeling immortal if only for a matter of minutes.

She was clinging to him as he spilled into her, and when he felt her climax his body went into overdrive as her heat swelled him and milked him like a gentle machine propelled by nothing more than mutual need.

But it wouldn't end there. The storm had just begun to settle when she raised her head. Rotating her hips on him, she said, "Anything that feels this good should become a habit, or maybe it has to do with the perfect fit. What do you think?"

"I think you're in the driver's seat."

She smiled, touched his cheek, then bent and kissed him. "Care to take another spin around the block? By the feel of things, you're up for it. Objections?"

"I can't think of any."

She was right, they were a perfect fit in more ways than one. And she was right about something else, too. Lightning did strike twice, and this time the storm raged for an hour.

Jaz wrapped her arms around his neck as he carried her to the bed and tucked her in. She had partied hard, as they say, only it hadn't been on too much wine. The truth was she'd gorged herself on too much of a good thing, and Ash Kelly was that good thing.

She wasn't going to get all starry-eyed and crazy. They'd had sex. Great, thunderstorm sex, and she was grateful to Ash for that, and so much more.

She was beginning to feel that if there was a way to fix this, he would find it.

"Need anything?" he asked as he covered her with the sheet.

"No."

"Okay. You rest, and I'll be back soon."

"Where are you going?"

"Out for a smoke. I won't be gone long. When I get back, if you're still awake, we'll talk."

"Want to give me a hint about what so I can start preparing? My memory isn't too reliable, remember?"

He bent and kissed her. "I think you know more than you realize. It's up to me to ask the right questions. Trust me."

Trust me.

A few days ago she would have rejected that offer. No, a few hours ago. But now it was something she wanted, as much as she wanted to believe that there was some way for her to repair the damage she'd done to the SDECE.

She fell asleep the minute her head hit the pillow, and with it came a number of disjointed dreams—beginnings with no ends, and ends that had no foundation.

She was in a chair, her wrists strapped down, and her ankles manacled with iron. The room was bright, and the voice…it kept badgering her.

"No more," she pleaded, then moaned because the bright light hurt her eyes. She wanted the voice to go away and leave her alone. But it was always there, like a record being replayed over and over again.

She fought the dream, then succumbed to the face behind the voice—a face of an animal with unnatural eyes. The face, the voice, the parroting phrases.

"No more, Cyrus. Stop it, please, you're killing me. No more. Please, no more. Not again. No, don't do that again. Not that… Oh, God, please!"

"Jaz? Jaz, wake up."

She jerked awake, and when she saw Ash seated beside her she sat up quickly. She felt as if she'd just run a mile, and her chest was heaving with each breath she took.

"I fell asleep."

"Understandable. You're exhausted. I take it you were dreaming about Cyrus. You mentioned his name."

"He was doing it again."

He stroked her hair away from her face. "Doing what?"

"He keeps saying the same thing over and over. Making me repeat it." She grabbed her head. "If I get it wrong…"

"What happens if you get it wrong?"

"He hurts me."

"How does he hurt you?"

"I'm strapped in a chair, and there are all these wires. They're taped all over me. If I don't repeat the letters in the right order the wires hurt."

"Electric shock." He swore, then stood and walked away. When he turned around, he said, "Tell me about the letters."

"I don't remember them, but that's crazy. I know them. I know I do."

Jaz shivered and Ash sat back down and pulled her into his arms. "I'm sorry," he said.

She looked up at him. "You don't have anything to be sorry for."

"I'm sorry this happened to you."

"Cyrus called it 'antiterrorist conditioning'."

"There's been some studies done on regenerating agents. It's a process of pulling old data out and replacing it with new information. In order for us to know if that's what we're dealing with here, I'm going to have to get you back to the agency as soon as possible."

She pushed away from him. "I can't go back to the SDECE."

"Then I'll take you to Onyxx."

"Onyxx is NSA."

"I know."

"I thought you said you were working for the SDECE."

"I am now, but I was NSA a week ago."

"I don't understand."

"That's not important. The important thing is to get you into the hands of someone who knows how this regeneration works."

She shook her head. "No. I won't be a guinea pig in some laboratory again."

"I understand how you feel, but—"

"How could you? You have no idea what I went through. Hell, I don't even remember half of it."

"Once I find the disk, we'll—"

"The one I can't remember stealing." Jaz felt like her entire world was coming apart. "I would never commit treason."

He stood. "But you did, honey. You just don't remember doing it."

Jaz buried her face in her hands. Suddenly, she realized

something, and she brought her head up slowly. "That's your mission? Recover the disk I stole, and then what?"

He hesitated and that's when she knew what his answer was going to be.

"Recover the disk data, and…you."

"Then that's why I'm here. You need me to find the disk."

"The disk isn't intact anymore. The minute you stole it it started to self destruct. On top of that it was encrypted. The SDECE thinks it vaporized before it could be decoded. It could be the case. There hasn't been any terrorist activity directed at them. But Stillman thinks it's still out there. Is it?"

"How do I know? I can't even remember stealing it."

"Salavich is a decoder. You're here with Filip. Those odds are hard to refute."

"Is Stillman your commander now?"

"Yes."

"Then call him and let me talk to him," Jaz suggested.

"Not a good idea."

"Why?"

"Because he's written you off as a traitor, and he'll send someone after you if I refuse to bring you in."

"And you're refusing?"

"At the moment, yes."

All of her trust in Ash Kelly suddenly died. "You've been playing me from the beginning."

"No." He came back and sat on the edge of the bed. "In the beginning I thought you were Allegra Nightingale."

"You lied to me."

"I never lied."

"You think I'm a traitor just like Stillman does. And Chanler."

"You don't believe that. You know what I think. I just can't prove it at the moment. I'm not going to sell you out, or turn you over until I have all the facts." He reached out to touch her, but she backed away.

"You're going to have to trust me, Jaz. I'm all you've got."

"And what if you don't find the data on that disk?"

"I'll find it."

"Not if I can't remember what I did with it." She was so frustrated she wanted to scream. Softly, she said, "Either way, I'll still be a traitor in the eyes of the SDECE. If you bring me back, the best I can hope for is that they'll kill me quick, but they won't. They'll lock me away."

He was back on his feet again, this time pacing the room. He was becoming as frustrated as her now. "It's a mess, but like I said, I'm working on it."

"I can't live in a cell."

That stopped him in his tracks. He was looking at her now, but his thoughts were somewhere else, and she knew where. He'd spent time in prison and he knew what it was like.

"You've been in a cage. I don't know why you were there, or how you became an agent, but you know what prison life feels like, and you know what happens to agents who are branded a traitor and locked up. I'm twenty-eight years old." Her heart was racing. "My bones will be picked daily, as well as my brain."

"What are you asking?"

"Promise me that you won't let that happen. Promise me that if this can't be fixed you'll do what needs to be done."

"And what is that?"

"Promise me that you'll kill me."

Merrick landed in Washington, and drove past his apartment building on his way to Sarah Finny's flower shop. It was past midnight, but he didn't care, he needed to see her.

When he'd phoned her from Paris and found out she was alive and unharmed, he'd felt such relief that he had collapsed in a chair. It had taken him several seconds to regain his voice, and when he had, he was sure that Sarah had sensed his fears.

She'd told him that she'd taken Cleo, the cat, home with her because she thought she was lonely. That she'd heard about the apartment fire, and that she was sorry.

Merrick parked his car and crossed the street. He saw no lights on above the flower shop. She was probably asleep. He rang the doorbell anyway.

The intercom light came on several minutes later, then he heard her voice.

"Yes, who is it?"

"Adolf. Can I come up, Sarah?"

"Adolf? Ah…of course. Come up."

The safety door made a click. Merrick swung it open and took the steps two at a time. He didn't have to knock. She had the door open when he reached the landing, standing there barefoot wearing a sexy pale yellow robe over a flimsy nightgown.

"I know it's late, but I just got in from the airport."

"It's all right. Come in."

He stepped inside. It was the second time he'd been in her apartment. She'd cooked him dinner one night months ago.

He took off his coat, and she took it from him and hung it on the coat tree. She headed into the kitchen and turned on the light.

"Would you like something to drink, or maybe you're hungry?" She turned around and that's when he knew he'd made a mistake coming up.

"Sarah, I…I shouldn't have stopped by so late. I just wanted to make sure you were all right."

The cat meowed, and he glanced down as the orange tabby rubbed against his pant leg.

"She's wonderful, Adolf. Pick her up. She likes to be cuddled."

He picked her up, and the cat started to purr like a motor.

"I've named her Cleo. I hope you like it."

"It's fine. It fits," he said, setting the cat back on the floor. "Sarah…"

"Come sit down."

"I don't want to sit down." He said the words too loudly and she flinched. "I'm sorry. I've just had a bad day all the way around."

"I understand."

"No, you don't. That's why I'm here. To make you understand why I can't see you anymore."

Ash had convinced Jaz that she needed to rest, and she finally fell asleep. While she slept, Ash stood at the window in the bedroom and waited for the signal.

When he saw it, he turned and reached for his gun on the nightstand.

A man who would go to such lengths as Cyrus had was a man who played to win. That meant he knew where Jaz was now.

Ash had played similar games in Mexico, and what he'd learned was that you always had a backup plan. Which meant he would be getting company real soon.

Ash walked to the bedroom door, opened it, then looked back. She was sleeping on her side, one arm raised over her head, her wrist handcuffed to the bedpost. She wouldn't be happy with him when she woke up. But she was too important to lose now. Important to his mission, and to him.

Promise me that if this can't be fixed you'll do what needs to be done. Promise me that you'll kill me.

He wasn't going to be able to promise her that, because he wasn't going to give up until she had her life back.

Like clockwork, Filip Petrov breached the infrared sensor Ash had installed outside the cabin while he was having a smoke. The minute the light went on, Ash positioned himself, and then Petrov touched the doorknob. The miniexplosive went off a second later and the door swung open just as Filip Petrov was lifted off his feet and blown off the deck onto his back. He struggled to get back on his feet, but the explosion had dazed him and he never made it before Ash stepped through the door, aimed his gun and shot him in the leg.

"I would have aimed higher," Naldo said as he appeared out of the shadows and picked up Filip's gun that had been dropped in the snow on impact as he'd been pitched backward fifteen feet.

"Dead men don't give answers," Ash said. "Help me get him over to the next cabin."

Twenty minutes later Filip was tied to a chair in the second bungalow Naldo had rented for Ash.

After his cousin tossed water in Petrov's face and the man started to come around, Ash stepped forward and drove his fist into Filip's jaw. The force snapped his head back and he moaned loudly.

"That's just the beginning," Ash said, "I'm going to take you apart a piece at a time, you sonofabitch. I want you to feel her pain."

He hit Petrov again. This time he broke his nose.

Chapter 13

While Filip was passed out, Ash called Sly. "Sly, it's Ash."

"Where the hell are you?"

"I'm close by, and things are shaping up like I planned. So far anyway. It's time for you to fly."

"Fly where?"

"Take Chanler to Stillman." Ash waited for Sly to say something. "I know you're not happy with the way I'm doing this job, but she's not a traitor, Sly. When this is all over, I'll be able to prove it."

"So you want me to deliver Chanler to Stillman in Paris."

"Then fly back here and wait to hear from me again. You should be able to get back by tomorrow afternoon, right?"

"If that's what you need, I'll be back."

"Thanks, Sly."

"Merrick wants you to give him a call."

"Okay."

"Are you going to do it?"

"I said I would."

"I'll wait to hear from you tomorrow."

When Ash hung up, Naldo said, "Now what?"

"Now we wake this sonofabitch up and he starts singing."

"What if you don't find out what you want to know?"

"Then we keep on him until he cracks. I'll get what I need from him one way or another."

"Not if he never wakes up. Hell, *primo*, I've never seen you go after a man like that before. What were you thinking?"

Ash faced his cousin. "He beat her up."

"Grant?"

"She's got more bruises on her body than a zebra's got stripes."

It was true he had gotten carried away, but every time Ash had hit Petrov he'd envision another bruise on Jaz's body.

"How is she doing?"

"She's been through hell, and there's still more to come. The problem is, I don't know how this is going to turn out."

When Naldo said nothing, Ash arched an eyebrow. "Go ahead and say it."

"She's a beautiful woman. If you would have let me spend more time with her it could have been me. I always said you were a one-woman man, even when you were tomcattin'." Naldo sobered. "Do you love her, *primo?*"

"I care about her."

"Care, as in wanting more than one night with her?"

"She's in a helluva mess, and if I can't prove she was used, she has no future."

"Then you'll prove it."

Filip moaned, and Ash turned his focus back to the business at hand. He stepped forward, and said, "Good, you're awake. Now that you understand how serious I am, tell me how you knew where to find Nightingale. And don't say it was a wild guess."

Naldo pulled out his knife. "A wrong answer, Señor Petrov, will bring you more pain. I think you've had enough pain to last a lifetime, no?"

"You don't know what you're asking," Filip muttered, his jaw swollen.

"I know exactly what I'm asking. You think if you tell me, then Cyrus will have no choice but to kill you." Ash smiled. "I wouldn't worry about him. I'm the only one you have to worry about right now. I don't like men who beat up women, and I'm anxious to continue proving that to you. Of course, I could be persuaded to give it a rest if I start getting answers to my questions. Keep in mind, I never repeat myself. Now we're going to start again, so listen carefully. Is she wearing a tracker?"

"Yes."

"Where?"

"I don't know."

"Wrong answer, *señor.*" Naldo stepped forward and ran his hand over the blade of his favorite knife.

"It's the truth. I don't know."

Ash pulled a small charge of explosives from his pocket. "You know what this can do. It can close a hole, or make one. It's all in the charge. I know a lot about explosives. Over the years it's made me a lot of money, so I've spent time perfecting my craft. Where's the data on the disk?"

Filip hesitated. "She has it. Nightingale has it."

Ash hoped to hell that wasn't true. At the moment she couldn't even remember stealing it.

The look on his face must have warned Petrov he didn't like his answer. Quickly, Filip said, "It's in her head."

That suddenly shed new light on the situation. Ash remembered Jaz saying she'd memorized letters.

"How do you access the data?"

"I don't know what you mean."

"I mean, if she's carrying around something she doesn't know she has, then there must be a way to access it. A word, or a phrase. A drug. Something that will trigger a response."

"Who the hell are you? No drug dealer I know thinks like that."

"You know who I am. If you want me to confirm that, I just did. Too bad it won't do you any good where you're going. When are you supposed to bring her to Salavich for decoding?"

"Tomorrow at ten o'clock in Salavich's office. I'm supposed to call…Cyrus when I've recovered Nightingale."

"Then we'll give him a call. And tomorrow?"

"I make another call and…Cyrus gives Nightingale what she needs to trigger her memory. She recites the code and from there Salavich deciphers it and e-mails it back to the Chameleon, I mean…"

Ash angled his head. "Did you say the Chameleon?"

"I meant Cyrus."

Ash was smiling now. "Cyrus is the Chameleon."

Filip closed his eyes. "I'm dead."

"You don't look so good, *señor,*" Naldo said, "but you're not dead."

Ash weighed the information. Jaz had the data, but without the ability to retrieve it, they were still out in the cold.

"What happens after the information has been decoded?"

"I send her to Athens."

"Back to the Chameleon?"

Filip never answered.

"I want a number where I can reach him."

"No. He's going to kill me."

Naldo poked his knife into Filip's neck. "Maybe not. Maybe I'll do it for him."

"It's programmed into my phone under Cyrus."

Ash took the phone from Filip's pocket and found the number. Then he sat down and took out his own phone. He had an idea, and it just might work. A half hour later, he was on his way out the door.

"I'll talk to you in the morning, Naldo. Make sure he stays put."

"Wait! What's going to happen to me?"

"That depends on whether you told me everything. If I don't come back alive, then my cousin will kill you. I'm sure you've figured out by now that he's as good with a knife as I am with explosives."

* * *

Jaz sat propped up against the headboard. It had been well over an hour since she'd been jerked awake by an explosion outside. It had been followed by a single gunshot.

She glared at the iron handcuff that kept her prisoner on the bed. Trust me, he'd said.

What about him trusting her?"

As much as he claimed to believe her, he'd just proven to her that he didn't.

She'd been a fool. She had fallen head over heels for every part of his con, including the false concern he'd shown her, and the seduction that had followed in the whirlpool.

He was good. She would give him that.

Bastard.

And now she was chained like an animal to a bedpost somewhere in the woods.

She heard a door bang shut and she waited. When ten minutes passed, she wondered if someone else other than Ash had entered the house. Another five minutes passed, then her jailer stepped into the room.

"You're awake."

"I woke up to an explosion and a gunshot. I called for you—" she raised her wrist "—after I couldn't get up."

"Sorry I had to do that. I needed to make sure you were safe."

That was crap, but she didn't warn him that she was on to him. "Has something happened?"

"Filip showed up."

"How did he find me so soon? Where is he now?"

"One question at a time." He walked to the bed, laid his gun on the table beside the bed, then pulled a key from his pocket and unlocked the handcuffs. "I figured he'd show."

She eyed his gun. "How?"

When she started off the bed, he stopped her. "I need to examine you."

"What?"

"You're wired with a tracking device. I thought that might be the case. Filip confirmed it."

"The bracelet."

"No. I just checked it. It was wired with explosives. It's at the bottom of the whirlpool now."

"Cyrus told me to never take it off."

"My guess is he was planning on getting rid of you if this went sour. What's wrong? You're awfully quiet."

"I'm just processing the information."

He stood and turned his back on her. In that split second, she reached for his gun, pulled the sheet around her and stood. "You're very good, Ash Kelly."

He heard her pull back the hammer and he spun around. "What are you doing?"

"I'm doing the only thing I can do. I'm leaving here. Get on the bed, and strap that handcuff on your wrist."

He made no move to do what she told him to do. "Was I wrong?"

"Wrong about what?" she asked.

"Are you a traitor?"

"No. But you don't believe me, and I can't trust you any longer."

"Because I used the handcuffs on you?"

"Waking up chained to the bed does kill one's trust."

"I told you why I did it."

Jaz didn't want to talk anymore. She was tired of him trying to sell himself to her. "Get on the bed." She motioned for him to walk around the opposite side of the bed. "Do it. Get on the bed."

He rounded the end of the bed and sat down on the mattress. Clamping the handcuff on his wrist, he said, "Come on, Jaz. This is all wrong. You just spent an hour making love with me, honey. I've got a plan, and it could work."

"Now he has a plan that could work."

"I know where the disk is, and I think I know where the tracker is, too."

"Where?"

"You're wearing the tracker."

She shook her head. "Nice try. I'm wearing nothing but a sheet."

"My money's on one of your cheek implants."

That piece of news gave her pause, and she put her hand to her right cheek and began to probe it. If it was there, she would surely feel it. After a few seconds, she felt the abnormality, a small hard pea just below her cheekbone. She touched the left cheek, and found another hard little lump.

"You found it, didn't you?"

"There's something in both of them," she said. "But they won't be there long. I'm going to cut them out."

"You can't alter anything until tomorrow. Not until we have the data."

"Cuff the bedpost."

"Dammit, Jaz!"

He did as she told him. Sprawled there, helpless, he glared at her. "You don't stand a chance without me."

She eased the hammer back on the gun and set it on the window ledge. "Unbuckle your belt."

"What?"

"Are you deaf? In the limo the first day I saw you, you unbuckled it one-handed. Come on, Ash, get to it."

He unbuckled his belt.

"Now unzip your jeans."

After he'd slid it down, she stepped to the foot of the bed and grabbed hold of the heel of one of his boots. Pulling it off, she moved on to the other one.

"Unbutton your shirt."

"Hell!"

"Do it."

It took him a few minutes, but he managed to work the buttons free.

"Now lift your ass."

When he did, she took hold of the hem of his jeans and jerk his pants off his hips and down his thighs. Working them off, she tossed them on the floor.

"How does it feel to be helpless?" she asked. "Chained up?"

"That depends on what's coming next."

"Why should I trust you?"

"Because I...I don't want anything to happen to you."

He said it like he meant it. Damn him for that.

"What do you know that you're not telling me?" she asked.

"I convinced Filip that it was in his best interest to talk. He sang like a bird."

"You said you know where the data is?"

"I do."

"Can we get it back?"

"If you're willing to trust me, we'll have it back by noon tomorrow."

"If you double-cross me, I'll—"

"Kill me. I know. You won't have to. Now get the key out of my pants pocket and unlock these cuffs."

Jaz shifted her eyes to his bare chest. "You said tomorrow morning?"

"That's right."

She dropped the sheet. "Then we have the night, and I have you right where I want you."

Ash watched her move toward the bed. She was so damn beautiful.

"What's going on?"

She walked to the bed and she climbed onto it. Leaning in, she kissed his chest, then teased one of his nipples with her lips.

His free hand curled around her bare back, and he moaned like a dying animal. "You scared the hell out of me."

She looked up. "Punishment for locking me up and making me think that you…"

"That I what?"

She looked away. "Nothing."

He cupped her chin and turned her face. "I believe you, and tomorrow, I'll prove to you that I'm a man you can trust."

Then he pulled her on top of him and kissed her like a man who was drowning. Happily drowning.

"Can we get rid of the cuffs now?"

* * *

In the middle of the night Ash woke up to find her gone. He rolled off the bed quickly, afraid that she had left him. He pulled on his jeans, and hurried into the living room to find her curled up in front of the fire on a blanket.

"What are you doing out here?"

She turned, and he saw tears on her cheeks. "Trying to remember."

He sat down on the blanket beside her. "Any luck?"

"Not much."

"About tomorrow. I think it's time I told you what's going to happen, and where the data from the disk is."

He told her what he'd learned from Filip. Explained his plan. Every detail, one step at a time.

"And the disk?"

Ash reached up and stroked her hair away from her face. "It's in here. You have it Jaz. It's all those letters you memorized."

"But I can't remember them."

"You will. Trust me."

"I want to. For the first time in my life, I want Bonnie to be wrong."

Ash smiled. "She had it rough. She taught you what she knew from experience. But maybe it's time you let go of her life, and started living your own."

"Will I ever be able to?"

"I'm trying to make that happen."

"Did you kill Filip?"

"No. Naldo's keeping him on ice."

"How did you ever get him to talk?"

"I used my charm. Filip's gay, you know."

Her eyes widened.

"You didn't know?"

She shook her head. "That's why he never touched me. He told me before we landed in Budapest that I was supposed to pretend that I was his woman, but—"

"He's lucky he never touched you, or I would have to break his arms…again."

"You hurt him?"

"Just a little." He pulled her close and kissed her forehead. "Come back to bed. You need sleep. Tomorrow, you're going to have to be at the top of your game."

"I'd like to stay here a while. I like the fire."

"Do you want to be alone?"

She snuggled against him, looked up. "No. It feels good to be held."

When she fell asleep, Ash continued to hold her. In fact he didn't let go of her all night. He'd told her maybe it was time she started living her own life. Maybe it was time he took his own advice.

Chapter 14

She wasn't in his arms when Ash woke up, and again a knot formed in his gut. But then he smelled the aroma of bacon frying, and he let out a relieved sigh.

He came to his feet, noticed that the fire had been fed. He walked into the kitchen and found her in his shirt standing in front of the stove.

He said, "She can cook."

She looked over her shoulder. "I like my eggs over easy. You?"

"That sounds good to me. How long have you been up?" He noticed her hair was wet. She'd been up long enough to shower.

"A few hours. You snore. Did you know that?"

"If you say so."

"We should go over your plan again. I have a few questions."

"There's time."

"I found some tea. If you—"

He came up behind her and wrapped his arms around her slender waist. "You could have left while I slept."

"As you pointed out last night, I have a tracker in my cheek." She turned around. "I wonder what's in the other one?"

"We'll find out soon."

All business this morning, she pushed his hands away and pulled down two plates from the cupboard. "The food's ready. If you're taking a shower, it'll have to wait."

She poured him a cup of water from the teapot, and then dropped a tea bag in and handed it to him. "To keep your hands busy."

He grinned. "New rules to go along with the new day?"

"We both need a clear head. You can be distracted easily. As you said last night, we need to be on top of our game today."

"You saying I can't keep up with you?"

"We'll see."

He ambled over to the table and sat. "So where did you learn to cook?"

"It was one of the things Bonnie taught me." She carried the plates to the table, then went back for the toast. She set the plate down in front of him and then sat across from him. "Juice?"

"I'm good with the tea, thanks."

She started to eat, and for a thin woman, she

seemed to enjoy the food this morning. She went after the bacon like she'd been deprived.

After the second bite, she closed her eyes and savored the burst of flavor. When she opened them and caught him staring, she said, "I haven't had bacon in months. At the base, I ate vegetables and lean protein. The meat… It was goat, I think. Once a day I was allowed fat, a pad of butter the size of a postage stamp."

"You said goat?"

"Yes."

The wheels started to turn in Ash's head. The Chameleon was still in Greece. "You said you don't remember where this compound is?"

"I was blindfolded when I left. The other times I don't remember."

"Because they were wiped out."

"Yes, I think so."

"When you left, did you fly out or go by boat?"

"Boat. The blindfold came off a few hours later. I was met in Athens and taken to Nescosto."

"To Yurii Petrov."

"I was there a few weeks before he arrived."

Ash finished his eggs and bacon, and sat back with his tea. "That must have been about the time he escaped from prison. The Chameleon knew he would. That means he was behind the jail break."

"I want to see Filip."

"To make sure he's alive?"

"No, to see how much damage you did."

"Not a good idea. I had Naldo pick you up some clothes." Ash motioned to the bag by the door. "As good as you look in my shirt and nothing else, you should probably change."

"It seems you're always buying me clothes. Thank you."

"Thank you for breakfast."

Ash's phone rang, and he set down his tea and stood. Phone to his ear, he said, "Where are you?"

"I just delivered Chanler to Stillman. Did you talk to Merrick?"

"I had to leave a message."

"Stillman wants to know if you've found the disk yet."

"Tell him I'm close. Did you tell him I've got Jaz with me?"

"No."

"Don't."

Jaz sat in the back of the limo next to Ash dressed in a black sweater and black pants. Ash was wearing jeans and his boots, his leather jacket hugging his broad shoulders.

The plan he'd laid out proved that he was a man who was as thorough in his job as he was in bed.

She watched him open the cupboard built into the console. He pulled out a small Beretta and handed it to her.

"Tuck that away."

She slipped it into the waistband of her pants and pulled the sweater over it just as Naldo was rounding the circle drive at Ballvaro.

Ash got out and Jaz followed him. Inside the bastion, the smell of smoke hung heavy in the air. It reminded Jaz of what had happened last night at Dominika's party. She hoped that she and Sophia were all right. She didn't have much use for Casso, but she did like his wife and daughter.

Two guards led them down a hall and opened Casso's office door. Stepping inside, she saw Salavich seated at his desk with another guard standing behind him.

"Mr. Toriago, this is a surprise. Where is Filip?"

"Filip is under the weather today, and he's asked me to represent him."

"I wasn't aware you two were close."

"He and I have a few things in common."

Ash grinned, as if he had just let his secret out of the bag. Jaz understood. He was suggesting that he was gay.

"I had no idea that you and Filip…well…" Casso turned his attention on Jaz. "Miss Nightingale, I'm glad to see that you are all right." His attention returned to Ash. "I'm afraid, Toriago, without Filip this meeting will not be possible. He has—"

"Given me the information. Like I said, he and I have become…friends."

Casso stood. "You must think I'm a fool."

"On the contrary, I think you're a very smart man," Ash said. "You're also in need of money."

"You seem to know a lot for a man who has recently come to Budapest, Toriago."

Jaz glanced at the clock; it was almost ten. "I have a scheduled flight back to Athens that leaves in an hour. We do this now, or we don't do it at all. Then you can explain to Cyrus why it didn't happen."

Salavich glared at Jaz. "Either you are a stupid woman, or very brave."

"I wouldn't be working for Cyrus if I was stupid."

"You are nothing but a courier."

Ash cleared his throat. "Are we ready to proceed?"

Casso glanced at his guards. "Step into the hall. Leave the door open. If either one of them tries to leave, kill them."

The guards moved quickly. Casso sat back down and hit a button on his keypad, while Jaz slipped into the chair in front of his desk. Ash flipped open Filip Petrov's cell phone, touched a button on the keypad, and set it down on the desk.

The Chameleon's voice filled the room. "I'm here, Filip."

Ash took his phone from his pocket, hit a record button, and Filip's voice came over the sound waves. "I'm here with Salavich, ready to decode, Cyrus."

Cyrus said, "Salavich?"

When Casso hesitated, Ash pulled his Beretta from his pocket and aimed it at him.

"Yes, Cyrus?"

"Are you ready?"

He sat back. He didn't look like he was going to answer at first. Finally, he said, "I'm ready."

"Where's Nightingale?"

"I'm here, Cyrus," Jaz answered.

"*Kalimera*, Nightingale."

"Good morning," she answered, and in that instant she remembered the letters in their proper order and they began to spill from her mouth like a fountain.

Ash stepped behind the desk and watched Casso Salavich's chubby fingers racing across the keyboard.

The minute Jaz stopped reciting the letters, he gave her a nod that Casso had gotten down what she'd recited. The room now quiet, she stood and went to the sideboard and poured a glass of water. Sipping the water, she returned to the desk and switched off both phones.

It took Salavich another ten minutes, and then he sat back with a heavy sigh. "I've got it."

Ash leaned over and studied the information on the screen. Stillman was right. The information would destroy the SDECE. It was all the access codes to every department within the organization.

He slid his hand into his pocket and triggered a mini-detonating device. Seconds later an explosion outside rattled the house. Casso started to get up, but Ash shoved him back into his chair, pressing the barrel of the gun into the fat man's neck.

"Send the guards outside to investigate that noise," he ordered quietly. He pressed the cold steel to a thick fold on Salavich's neck. "Go on, send them away."

"Joey, take the men and see what's happening outside. Go quickly!"

As the men scrambled down the hall to follow their boss's orders, Jaz set the glass of water on the desk, then went and closed the door.

"You're never going to get away with this," Casso promised. "You have no idea who you're dealing with."

"And neither do you," Ash said. "Get on your feet."

Casso stood slowly.

"Over here in this chair," Jaz said, her gun now drawn, to persuade him to move.

Casso did what he was told. "You won't get out of here alive."

Ash ignored Casso's threat and quickly sat down at the desk and made a disk of the information on the screen. He then slipped the disk in his pocket and pulled a handful of pea-size explosives from his pocket and tossed them on the computer's keypad. As he rounded the desk, he grabbed the glass of water and tossed it on the computer. The minute the liquid made contact with the red-hots, as Ash called them, the computer began to short out, then expel a putrid smell.

"No!" Casso screamed. "You have no idea what you've just done. Years of work. Billions gone!"

Ash grinned. "Did you say gone? That doesn't sound good. Especially for a man who's been having money problems lately. Your enemies will be celebrating shortly, I imagine."

"Bastard!"

Casso tried to get up, but Jaz shoved him back in his chair. When Casso opened his mouth in protest, Ash jammed a small rubber ball in it, then jerked the overweight man back to his feet.

Cuffing his hands behind his back, he led Salavich to the closet and shoved him inside. "Now if I were you, I wouldn't move until one of your men finds you. That ball is real touchy. A little too much pressure and you just might go boom."

The minute Casso's eyes widened, Ash shut the door.

"That was a little extreme, wasn't it?" Jaz asked.

"What? It was just a rubber ball. Come on, we're out of here."

"That's going to be difficult now that you blew up the limo."

"It's toast."

"Then how are we getting out of here? You never did explain that part of the plan."

"The hard way. Stay close."

He moved into the hall with Jaz close behind him. Ash heard a shot behind him and he turned to see that Jaz had taken out a guard.

He started into the foyer, when she said, "Not that way."

He spun around and quickly followed her down another hall.

"Where's Naldo?" she asked.

"He's waiting for us at the helicopter pad."

"Can he fly it?"

"That's the plan."

A gunshot ricocheted off the wall and missed Ash by less than an inch. "We have to get outside or we're going to get trapped." When they reached the sweeping staircase, Jaz started up.

"What the hell are you doing? I said out, not up."

"Up then out."

She shot the guard at the top of the stairs, and then spun around and shot two more that had taken chase.

It was a sight to see, her in action. Jaz was like a machine, her moves so damn automatic Ash was speechless.

She said, "Call Naldo and tell him to get the helicopter in the air."

"What!"

"Tell him to secure a rope and toss it out, then take off. Do it!"

On the run, Ash pulled out his phone and called his

cousin while Jaz shot two more guards. Naldo was sure he hadn't heard right, and Ash repeated the order. They had reached the second staircase when they heard the chopper winding up. Still moving like hell on fire, Jaz didn't slow down when she started up the third staircase. Taking the steps two at a time she easily kept ahead of Ash while he was doing double time to keep up.

"What's your holdup? Come on, Boy Scout."

Puffing, Ash yelled, "Where are we going?"

"To the roof."

She had to be crazy, he thought, as they reached the fourth floor. That's when she really kicked it in as she raced down the hall and through a door. More steps, and these she took at the same breakneck speed, flying up the stairs like she was a bird being carried on the wind.

She opened another door, and they came out on the roof. Naldo was in the air now, and Ash called him and gave him their location.

A volley of gunfire warned him that they'd been spotted, and he grabbed Jaz and shoved her behind him. They were pinned down and he knew that Naldo was going to see some action soon. He'd be shot down if they didn't make a move.

"How well do you climb?" she asked.

Ash glanced at her. "This isn't a good time to tell me you can't."

She grinned, then said, "Tell Naldo to move in. There's only one rope, remember? We need to grab it both at the same time. On three I'll go high, you go low."

The door behind them blew off its hinges, and the

second the noise registered, Jaz rolled to her side and shot the guard before Ash blinked.

"Hell, woman."

She grinned. "Better not get me mad."

"I'll remember that."

Ash called Naldo and the helicopter made a wide sweep and started toward the roof. The helicopter flew over them, and on the count of three, they grabbed the rope. Seconds later the guards on the ground unloaded a pound of lead at the helicopter.

Ash looked up to see where Jaz was. He found her halfway up the rope when disaster struck.

He saw her take the hit. Then she let go of the rope.

"I'm sorry, Stillman, Grant didn't make it. She's dead."

"Dead?"

Ash had flown into Paris four hours after he'd recovered the disk. He pulled it from his pocket, then took a seat in front of Stillman's desk. "I did manage to recover this." He handed it to the SDECE commander, then sat back and crossed his leg over his knee and lit a cigarette.

"You recovered the disk! Wonderful."

"About Grant."

Stillman sat back in his chair. "Yes, what about her?"

"She was shot while I was trying to escape with her from Ballvaro."

"Did you get a chance to talk to her and find out why she did it? I still can't believe she turned traitor on us."

"She didn't. I know Chanler's convinced that's what she is, and you, too. But the truth is she was captured and brainwashed. She wasn't herself when she stole that disk. She had no idea she'd even done it until I told her. She helped me recover the data to prove herself to you."

"And you believe her motives were pure?"

"I wouldn't have gotten the disk back without her help. She went through hell."

Stillman stood and turned his back. He rubbed his neck, considered what he'd heard.

Ash waited for some sign, some kind of appreciation. Loyalty. Admiration. What he got left him cold.

"It's just as well that she's dead. I could never bring her back to the SDECE. It would have been a messy ordeal. Chanler, I can explain. I've figured out how to bring him back, but Grant... No, she'll be missed, but it's better this way."

Ash did all he could do to stay seated. "It's all about you, isn't it? It would be too messy for you."

Stillman spun around. "Have you been in contact with Merrick?"

"No, not yet. But I will be shortly. As far as this goes, I don't need anyone to draw me a picture. There are some things that a man can figure out for himself. It was your negligence that put Jaz Grant back in the hands of the enemy. If you want someone to blame for this, look in the mirror."

"She was my best agent. I needed her back in the field. I took a gamble and I lost. You're sure she's dead?"

"Yes. I want her record clean. I don't want one blemish on it."

"Of course. With her dead, there is no reason anyone should know about this."

"I thought you'd see it my way." Ash stood.

"Where are you going?"

"Back to Onyxx. I did what you asked. And I figure since I know more than I should, you'd prefer to have me as far away from here as possible."

"Are you blackmailing me?"

"I cleaned up your dirty business, Stillman. You owe me my freedom. I'll take it now, or I'll see you on the street with a broom."

Stillman sat back down. "The disk is back, and Grant's dead."

"And you're off the hook."

Stillman narrowed his eyes. "I'm a good commander. I made one mistake."

"And it cost you the best agent you ever had. If she would have lived, what would you have done to her?"

"You know what happens to traitors in this business, Kelly. Whether she was willing or not, she could never be trusted again. I would have liked to have seen her one last time. But you answered a few of my questions, and I'll have to live with what I'll never know. She really was a good agent."

"Yes, she was."

Ash called Merrick from Paris. He had a lot to tell him and most of it was good news.

"This is Merrick."

"It's Ash."

"Is it over?"

"Just about. I've got some things to tell you, and I wanted you to know as soon as possible."

"Know what?"

Ash told Merrick how it had gone down at Ballvaro. He filled in the holes about the escape, and went over his meeting with Stillman. "He's letting me go. I'm back at Onyxx again if you want me."

"Damn right I want you."

"I have some good news for you."

"I can always use good news."

"Cyrus is the Chameleon and he's still in the Greek Isles. Start looking at the islands that are about four hours away from Athens by boat."

Silence.

"Merrick?"

A quieter Adolf Merrick said, "Good work, Ash. Damn good work. What about Filip Petrov?"

"Sly should have picked him up by now. After he delivered Chanler to Stillman, I asked him to return to Budapest and pick up Petrov. He's headed back to Washington."

"I have a piece of good news for you, too. Stillman was bluffing about knowing where your family is. They're still safe."

"Thanks, Merrick. I'll see you soon."

Chapter 15

"How are you feeling today, *señorita?* How is your arm?"

Jaz turned to see Naldo standing on the grand balcony of the home he shared with the Toriago family south of Girona, Spain. It had been a week since Ash's cousin had brought her home with him.

She was lucky to be alive, and Ash Kelly was responsible for that. He'd plucked her out of midair like a guardian angel after she'd been shot. The wound wasn't serious, but it had caught her by surprise and she'd made an almost fatal mistake.

"Have you heard from Ash?"

"No. But don't worry. He will call when he finds a safe place for you."

"Call?"

"*Sì.*"

"Will he come for me then?"

"No. I will take you there."

When he finds a safe place for you.

"Do you know if he returned the data to the SDECE?"

"I know that was his plan."

She touched her cheeks where the tracker and a sonar chip had been removed the same day she had arrived in Girona. The surgeon had done a good job. Naldo had explained that the man doing the surgery was someone the Toriago family trusted.

She knew she should be grateful to Ash for what he'd done for her—what he was now doing—finding a safe place for her. And she was; she just couldn't help feeling a little angry about how they had parted company. The minute the helicopter had landed after their escape, he'd leapt out, motioned for Naldo to take off again, and then he was gone without a word.

No goodbye.

No last look.

Nothing.

It was then that she realized her life as she knew it was over. She had no home, no country and no job.

She turned to look out over the *Matro* vineyard. Ash's mother, Elnora, said it meant "God's gift." It was a gift all right. The villa was beautiful. It sat on a hillside overlooking acres and acres of flourishing green vineyards.

She wondered if she had ever been to Spain before, if she would ever remember her entire life from start to finish. Probably not. It was gone…and so was Ash.

She hated that part most of all. Those last few days he'd become her reason for living. Against all Bonnie's warnings, she'd found a man she respected and could trust.

A man she could love.

Did love.

"*Señorita?*"

"Yes?"

"I said, Robena was wondering if you felt up to going shopping with her today? She's looking for the most beautiful wedding dress in Barcelona."

Ash's sister was a dark-eyed beauty with a friendly smile and a curious mind. For the past week she had been asking Jaz a dozen questions a day, and they all centered around her brother. It was obvious that Robena loved and respected Ash. But then who wouldn't love and respect him? He was the Boy Scout.

Just yesterday Robena had said, "Six years ago my *hermano* sacrificed everything for *madre* and me. Naldo, too. He is the reason we are here. The reason *madre* is happy again, and I have found the man I will marry. He is the reason we exist at all."

"*Señorita?*"

She turned. "Tell Robena I would love to go shopping with her. I'll get ready."

Within the hour they were all driving to Barcelona, Naldo and Elnora in the front seat and Robena and Jaz in the back. They shopped all morning, and then ate lunch at a seaside restaurant. Naldo said he and Elnora had some vineyard business to take care of and so she and Robena continued on without them in search of "the most beautiful wedding dress in the city."

By late afternoon, they had found the dress, and Robena had been fitted. She was getting married in less than six weeks, and she was the happiest bride-to-be Jaz had ever met. Well, perhaps the only bride-to-be she'd ever met.

Naldo and Elnora rejoined them in the late afternoon. "I thought we would have dinner at *Loret de Mara*. It is on the road home, and the sunset will be beautiful," Naldo said.

Elnora said the resort was one of the most popular on the coast, and Jaz could see why when they arrived. It was magnificent.

"Look," Naldo said, "A yacht show at the marina. I have always wanted a big boat. Come, let's look."

"After dinner," Robena begged.

"I think it would be fun," Jaz said.

"*Estoy cansado*, Naldo," Robena argued, "my feet are killing me."

Elnora suggested, "We'll go get a table and the two of you enjoy the show, then join us when you're finished."

It didn't take Naldo but a moment to agree to the idea, and he grabbed Jaz's hand and pulled her along to find his dream boat. He spotted it ten minutes later as he headed down the dock.

"Is she not the most beautiful boat in port, *señorita?*"

Jaz nodded. "You have expensive taste, Naldo."

"Let's look inside. I have always wanted a party boat."

Jaz laughed as they boarded the 90-foot dream boat. It looked wicked and fast for a yacht, and yet belowdecks it had all the comforts of home—two spacious staterooms with bathrooms in each, a living area, and a kitchen.

"Check out this shower, *señorita,*" Naldo called out to her.

Jaz was in the kitchen, and she headed down the companionway to see the master stateroom's elegant gold and marble bathroom with an oversized shower.

Naldo left the bathroom and began to drool over the big king-size bed.

When she left the bathroom he was standing in the doorway that led back down the companionway.

She said, "We better get back to Elnora and Robena before they come looking for us."

"I think instead you should take a nap."

Jaz frowned. "A nap?"

He stepped backwards, and before she realized what he was about to do, he pulled the door shut.

"Naldo, stop goofing around." She walked to the door, but before she reached it she heard a loud click—he'd locked her inside.

"Naldo!" She grabbed the knob and tried to open the door. "Naldo! This isn't funny."

"I'm sorry, *señorita.* I was serious about the nap. An hour should be about right."

"Naldo, open this door!"

In a matter of minutes she heard the yacht's twin engines start up. She raced to the window and looked out. The yacht was leaving port. She tried to open one of the windows, but they were all locked.

Then she remembered what Naldo had told her earlier that morning. *He'll call when he finds a safe place for you. I'll take you there.*

Jaz could only come up with one good reason why Naldo had locked her below deck. Wherever he was taking her, she wasn't going to like it.

She paced the stateroom, considering a location that could be reached by boat that would take an hour from Barcelona. She was close to France. Maybe Stillman had decided to meet her. Or perhaps she was going to be dumped off on a remote island.

It was over an hour when the engines shut down and the yacht docked. Jaz peered out the window and saw that Naldo had pulled the boat into a small port on a beautiful sandy island.

Island...

The Balearic Islands were southeast of Barcelona.

Is that where they were?

She heard him unlock the door. But he didn't come in. That was smart of him because right now if she had a gun she would take his head off.

She opened the door and stepped out into the companionway. A quick search told her that he was back up on deck. She climbed the stairs and stepped into the warm sunlight and looked around. The island was a beachcomber's paradise, and the water was as clear and blue as the sky.

"This is just a stopping-off place, *señorita*."

She turned. "Where are we?"

"Formentera. It is beautiful, no?"

"Yes, it is."

He angled his head. "You are angry with me."

"I'm angry, but not at you."

"My *primo*?"

"Yes, your cousin. I wanted to see him one more

time, but I guess that was more important to me than
to him. When you see him, you can tell him that—"

"Why don't you tell me yourself?"

The sound of his voice sent Jaz's heart racing. She
turned slowly and there he was, standing on the docks
wearing jeans and a white shirt, with half the buttons
open.

He looked good. So good she almost forgot that
she was angry.

"Naldo."

"*Sì, primo.*"

"How does she handle?"

Naldo looked back at the yacht. "She's a beautiful
party boat."

Ash laughed. "She's yours. A little gift for your help
this past week."

Naldo sobered. "You're serious, *primo*?"

"I appreciate what you did in Budapest for us." He
glanced at Jaz, then back at his cousin. "Tell Robena
I'll be back for the wedding. I'll see you in five weeks."

Jaz was about to get off the boat when Naldo took
hold of her hand. Turning her to face him, he whispered, "It's been a wild ride, *señorita*. Good luck, and
don't be too angry with him."

He kissed her cheek, and then Jaz stepped off the
boat and Naldo disappeared into the cockpit. Seconds
later he was on his way back to Girona.

She looked different. Not back to the old Jaz in
Stillman's profile, but he could see that the cheek
implants were gone, and she was no longer wearing
green contacts.

Still, it was Jaz, the woman he'd been unable to forget from the moment he'd put her in the helicopter with Naldo and walked away.

"You had something you wanted to tell me?" he reminded.

"Where have you been?"

"To Paris to see Stillman, then to Washington."

"The SDECE has the data back?"

"They do."

"And me? What did Stillman say about me?"

Ash didn't want to have this conversation on the dock. He said, "Can we talk somewhere else?" He pointed to another yacht. "Let's talk on my boat."

"Your boat?" She turned around and saw a well-seasoned boat docked in the harbor. It wasn't as fancy as the one he'd bought for Naldo, but it was almost as big.

He headed down the dock with her walking a few steps behind him. Once they were on board, he gestured to a seat in the cockpit.

When she didn't sit, he said, "You can't go back to the SDECE."

"Stillman wants me dead, so you came to finish the job?"

Ash rubbed his jaw, considered how he should tell her. He decided to just say it. "I told him you didn't make it. That you died at Ballvaro recovering his disk."

"Why?"

"It was the only way for you to have a future, Jaz. It's better this way."

"Better for whom? Am I supposed to wait tables on this island for the rest of my life?"

"That would be a waste."

She turned away from him and looked out over the water. "Thanks for delivering the bad news in person."

"I wanted to see you."

She looked at him. "Well, now you have. You better get going."

She started out of the cockpit, but Ash grabbed her arm and stopped her. "We're not finished."

"More bad news."

"I don't think it is. I guess that all depends. You have a meeting with Adolf Merrick from Onyxx in a week in the Canary Islands."

"Are you working for Onyxx again?"

"Yes."

"What's the meeting about?"

"He's bringing a doctor with him. A specialist from Onyxx to examine you."

"How dare you hand me over like some freak experiment that's gone bad?"

"That's not what I'm doing. You've been inside one of the Chameleon's hideouts. You can provide information that might help us capture him. And I know you'd like that. After all, he put you through hell."

"What's the catch?"

"No catch. I told Merrick about your experience. He'd like to discuss a job offer. Of course you wouldn't be expected to jump right back on the horse. You'll need to work with the doctor for a while. You proved at Ballvaro that you're an excellent field operative, but Merrick thinks you might like teaching what you know. I told him I had trouble keeping up with you."

"You told him that?"

"Anyway, he thinks you'd be an asset to the training program at Onyxx."

Ash waited for her to say something, but when she turned away he was afraid she was going to turn it all down. If she said no to Onyxx, then she would sure as hell say no to his next idea.

And then what would he do?

She was looking out over the water again. Finally, she said, "Thank you. You said you would fix this, and you have. I'm grateful."

"How grateful?"

She turned around. "Very grateful."

"Grateful enough to move to Washington?"

"Is that where you live?"

"When I'm not working."

"So we would…see each other."

"My apartment isn't that big. I've never gotten lost in it once. Of course we could get something bigger if you want. The *señorita* finally smiles, and what a smile it is."

"You want me to move in with you?"

"I gave you a piece of advice in Budapest, then realized that I should be taking it myself. We should be with the person that makes us happy. Trust them, help them, and wake up next to them every day. I want that to be you, Jaz. Now if you don't feel the same—"

"Look in my eyes and tell me what you see."

Ash walked toward her and slowly wrapped his arms around her. Looking into her eyes, he said, "You care about me."

"Try again."

He drew in a deep breath, then let it out slowly. "You love me."

"He really can read eyes."

Ash tightened his hold on her and whispered, "You won't regret it."

She leaned back and cupped his face. "And you won't regret loving me. You do, don't you?"

"With every part of me."

She was smiling again. "Speaking of that. Naldo suggested I take a nap on the ride over here, but I never got around to it. Is there a bed belowdecks?"

"*Sì, señorita,* a nice big bed."

"And do you have a shower, too? The one in Naldo's yacht is huge."

Ash grinned. "Mine's bigger."

He leaned in and kissed her slow and deep. The future would be what they made of it. In a week the Canary Islands, then Robena's wedding, after that, on to Washington where he would wake up next to her every morning.

"I love you," he whispered, then suddenly he lifted her into his arms. "I think we should toast the future."

"You don't drink, Boy Scout."

"Exactly. I guess we're going to have to think of another way to celebrate. The bed first, or the shower?"

Epilogue

When the decoded data didn't reach him, the Chameleon knew he'd been conned. How it had happened he would never know exactly. Filip had disappeared without a trace. And Nightingale... He'd lost contact with her, too. Which meant the tracker had been discovered and removed from inside her cheek.

He'd smelled a rat—an Onyxx rat. And he'd been right. Somehow Merrick had become involved with the SDECE, and together they had recovered the data.

Months of work flushed down the toilet.

He wasn't used to losing. And in this particular situation Merrick's interference had cost him billions. He should have leveled more than just his apartment building.

He would think on that. Perhaps it was time that his

old friend knew the truth. After all, they had so much in common.

Perhaps it was time to end the game. Or at least raise the stakes.

The Chameleon pulled up his custom-made sniper, aimed the rifle over the rampart of the tower and looked through the scope. The movement in the rocks came into view seconds later and he squeezed the trigger.

His accuracy was as sharp and on-target as any assassin in the business. The goat dropped to its knees and was dead before it hit the ground.

He lowered the gun just as a scream was offered up to the heavens. He scanned the rocky terrain and saw Melita running down the uneven path toward the dead goat. She knelt beside the lifeless beast, then turned her head back to *Minare,* her eyes finding him standing in the tower.

"I hate you," she screamed.

That was nothing new, he thought as he studied his little Joan of Arc.

When she got back to her feet, he called down to her. "Get a guard to clean up that mess. Tell him to save the meat."·

The look on her face was priceless.

"What did you think you've been eating this past year, beef?"

She screamed at him again, like a young child throwing a tantrum. This time he laughed at her, then turned and went back inside.

Now what to do with Barinski? Did Dr. Frankenstein start over with a new guinea pig, or did he rid himself of the freak that had failed him? It was rare that he let anyone live once they had disappointed him.

He was still considering Barinski's fate when he met Melita in the hall, her face tear-stained and her hands covered in blood.

"Go clean yourself up. Dinner's at seven."

"I feel ill. I won't be hungry."

"I'm sure you'll feel better in a few hours."

Her eyes defied him, and then she raised her hands and smearing the goat's blood on his white shirt. "You disgust me."

He smiled down at her, enjoying her spirit. "Wear something pretty. One of the dresses Callia bought you in Naxos. I favor the blue one. Seven sharp."

She walked off, and he knew she'd be late. That's if she showed up at all.

Children. They did try a parent's patience. She would join him, however, if he had to hunt her down and drag her from her room by her lovely hair.

That's why he told the cook to serve the goat at eight.

* * * * *

A special treat for you from Harlequin Blaze!

Turn the page for a sneak preview of
DECADENT
by
New York Times *bestselling author*
Suzanne Forster

Available November 2006,
wherever series books are sold.

Harlequin Blaze—Your ultimate destination
for red-hot reads.
With six titles every month, you'll never guess
what you'll discover under the covers...

Run, Ally! Don't be fooled by him. He's evil. Don't let him touch you!

But as the forbidding figure came through the mists toward her, Ally knew she couldn't run. His features burned with dark malevolence, and his physical domination of everything around him seemed to hold her like a net.

She'd heard the tales. She knew all about the Wolverton legend and the ghost that haunted The Willows, an elegant old mansion lost by Micha Wolverton nearly a hundred years ago. According to folklore, the estate was stolen from the Wolvertons, and Micha was killed trying to reclaim it. His dying vow was to be reunited with the spirit of his beloved wife, who'd taken her life for reasons no one would speak of, except in whispers. But Ally had never put much stock in the fantasy. She didn't believe in ghosts.

Until now—

She still didn't understand what was happening. The figure had materialized out of the mist that lay thick on the damp cemetery soil. A cool breeze and silvery moonlight had played against the ancient stone of the crypts surrounding her, until they joined the mist, causing his body to thicken and solidify right before her eyes. That was when she realized she'd seen this man before. Or thought she had, at least.

His face was familiar. . . so familiar, yet she couldn't put it together. Not with him looming so near. She stepped back as he approached.

"Don't be afraid," he said. His voice wasn't what she expected. It didn't sound as if it were coming from beyond the grave. It was deep and sensual. Commanding.

"Who are you?" she managed.

"You should know. You summoned me."

"No, I didn't." She had no idea what he was talking about. Two minutes ago, she'd been crouching behind a moss-covered crypt, spying on the mansion that had once been The Willows, but was now Club Casablanca. And then this—

If he was Micha, he might be angry that she was trespassing on his property. "I'll go," she said. "I won't come back. I promise."

"You're not going anywhere."

Words snagged in her throat. "Wh-why not? What do you want?"

"If I wanted something, Ally, I'd take it. This is about need."

His words resonated as he moved within inches of her. She tried to back away, but her feet were useless. "And you need something from me?"

"Good guess." His tone burned with irony. "I need lips, soft and surrendered, a body limp with desire."

"My lips, my bod—?"

"Only yours."

"Why? Why me?" This couldn't be Micha. He didn't want any woman but Rose. He'd died trying to get back to her.

"Because you want that, too," he said.

Wanted what? A ghost of her own? She'd always found the legend impossibly romantic, but how could he have known that? How could he know anything about her? Besides, she'd sworn off inappropriate men, and what could be more inappropriate than a ghost? She shook her head again, still not willing to admit the truth. But her heart wouldn't play along. It clattered inside her chest. The mere thought of his kiss, his touch, terrified her. This wildness, it was fear, wasn't it?

When his fingertips touched her cheek, she flinched, expecting his flesh to be cold, lifeless. It was anything but that. His skin was smooth and hot, gentle, yet demanding. And while his dark brown eyes were filled with mystery and wonder, there was a sensitivity about them that threatened to disarm her if she looked too deeply.

"These lips are mine," he said, as if stating a

universal fact that she was helpless to avoid. In truth,
it was just that. She couldn't stop him.

And she didn't want to.

* * * * *

Find out how the story unfolds in...
DECADENT
by
New York Times *bestselling author*
Suzanne Forster.
On sale November 2006.

Harlequin Blaze—our ultimate destination
for red-hot reads.
With six titles every month, you'll never guess
what you'll discover under the covers...

nocturne™

HER BLOOD WAS POISON TO HIM...

MICHELE HAUF

FROM THE DARK

Michael is a man with a secret. He's a vampire
struggling to fight the darkness of his nature.
It looks like a losing battle—until he meets
Jane, the only woman who can understand his
conflicted nature. And the only woman who can
destroy him—through love.

On sale November 2006.

nocturne™

USA TODAY **bestselling author**

MAUREEN CHILD

ETERNALLY

He was a guardian. An immortal fighter of evil,
out to destroy a demon, and she was his next
target. He knew joining with her would make
him strong enough to defeat any demon.
But the cost might be losing the woman
who was his true salvation.

On sale November, wherever books are sold.

nocturne™

Save $1.⁰⁰ off

your purchase of any
Silhouette® Nocturne™ novel.

Receive $1.00 off

any Silhouette® Nocturne™ novel.

**Available wherever books are sold, including most
bookstores, supermarkets, drugstores and discount stores.**

Coupon expires December 1, 2006. Redeemable at participating
retail outlets in the U.S. only. Limit one coupon per customer.

5 65373 00076 2   (8100) 0 11265

SNCOUPUS

nocturne™

Save $1·⁰⁰ off

your purchase of any
Silhouette® Nocturne™ novel.

Receive $1.00 off
any Silhouette® Nocturne™ novel.

**Available wherever books are sold, including most
bookstores, supermarkets, drugstores and discount stores.**

Coupon expires December 1, 2006. Redeemable at participating
retail outlets in Canada only. Limit one coupon per customer.

RETAILER: Harlequin Enterprises Limited will pay the face value of this coupon
plus 10.25 cents if submitted by the customer for this specified product only. Any
other use constitutes fraud. Coupon is nonassignable. Void if taxed, prohibited or
restricted by law. Consumer must pay any government taxes. Mail to Harlequin
Enterprises Ltd., P.O. Box 3000, Saint John, New Brunswick E2L 4L3, Canada. Limit
one coupon per customer. Valid in Canada only.

52607136

SNCOUPCDN

REQUEST YOUR FREE BOOKS!

2 FREE NOVELS
PLUS 2
FREE GIFTS!

Passionate, Powerful, Provocative!

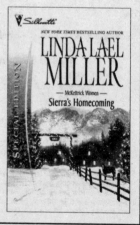

HARLEQUIN

Blaze

New York Times bestselling author
Suzanne Forster brings you
another sizzling romance...

Club Casablanca—an exclusive gentleman's club where
exotic hostesses cater to the every need of high-stakes
gamblers, politicians and big-business execs. No rules
apply. And no unescorted women are allowed. Ever.
When a couple gets caught up in the club's hedonistic
allure, the only favors they end up trading are sensual....

DECADENT

November 2006

by

Suzanne Forster

Get it while it's hot!

Available wherever series romances are sold.

"Sex and danger ignite a bonfire of passion."
—*Romantic Times BOOKclub*

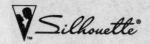

COMING NEXT MONTH

#1439 CLOSER ENCOUNTERS—Merline Lovelace
Code Name: Danger
Drew McDowell—Code name Riever—is curious to know why a recently fired defense attorney has developed a sudden interest in a mysterious WWII ship. When the mission takes a bizarre twist, the two must work together, while fighting an attraction that threatens to consume them both.

#1440 FULLY ENGAGED—Catherine Mann
Wingmen Warriors
Pararescueman Rick DeMassi never thought the woman he'd shared an incredible night with years ago would be his next mission. But when a stalker kidnaps her and his daughter, this air force warrior must face his greatest fears and save the two most important women in his life.

#1441 THE LOST PRINCE—Cindy Dees
Overthrown in a coup d'état, the future king of Baraq runs to the only woman who can help him. Now Red Cross aide Katy McMann must risk her life and her heart to help save a crumbling nation.

#1442 A SULTAN'S RANSOM—Loreth Anne White
Shadow Soldiers
To stop a biological plague from being released, mercenary Rafiq Zayed is forced to abduct Dr. Paige Sterling and persuade her to team up with him in a race against a deadly enemy...and their growing desires.